THE JUDGE'S TERRITORY

When Sam Gould first arrived in Conchas City, his abiding interest in its ailing newspaper forced him into conflict with a powerful local group, headed by a retired circuit judge, H. Dan Sherman. However, he worked off his early frustrations by doing an investigating job for the town lawyer, and when a former Pinkerton detective was murdered, Sam undertook a highly dangerous assignment for Judge Sherman. This took time, guts and a whole lot of risks, but Sam eventually won through.

Books by David Bingley
in the Linford Western Library:

THE BEAUCLERC BRAND
ROGUE'S REMITTANCE
STOLEN STAR
BRIGAND'S BOUNTY
TROUBLESHOOTER ON TRIAL
GREENHORN GORGE
RUSTLERS' MOON
SUNSET SHOWDOWN
TENDERFOOT TRAIL BOSS
HANGTOWN HEIRESS
HELLIONS' HIDEAWAY

DAVID BINGLEY

THE JUDGE'S TERRITORY

Complete and Unabridged

LINFORD
Leicester

First published in Great Britain in 1976

CRANFORD LIBRARY
First Linford Edition
published 2004

C206457B 2/05

British Library CIP Data

Bingley, David, *1920* –
The judge's territory.—Large print ed.—
Linford western library
1. Western stories
2. Large type books
I. Title II. Chatham, Larry, *1920* –
823.9′14 [F]

ISBN 1–84395–583–0

Published by
F. A. Thorpe (Publishing)
Anstey, Leicestershire

Set by Words & Graphics Ltd.
Anstey, Leicestershire
Printed and bound in Great Britain by
T. J. International Ltd., Padstow, Cornwall

This book is printed on acid-free paper

1

Sam Gould, for once, looked his twenty-five years as he moved away from the long bar of the Bonanza saloon, in the High Street of Conchas City, in the county of the same name, New Mexico territory. Clutched in his right hand, he had a tall glass of lukewarm beer. In the other, a couple of stogies and a few long match sticks. He moved to an empty table in the area away from the card players and settled himself down to drink and smoke.

Between twenty and thirty men, mostly locals, were sharing the saloon in the hour prior to noon. One or two groups looked over the youthful newcomer, but as he made no effort to get acquainted with anyone they soon lost interest and talked among themselves on other subjects.

Among other things, Sam was an

experienced traveller. He had a knack of shrugging off the curiosity of others when he was in a thoughtful mood and he was that way now. He had ridden into town around eight in the morning after spending the best part of a fortnight in the saddle, slowly making his way westward from Amarillo, in the Texas Panhandle.

His mind was in a turmoil of mixed feelings. He had been raised in Amarillo and most of his wanderings this far had been in Texas, Kansas, Colorado, and the territories of Oklahoma and New Mexico. As a youngster, he had worked on ranches when many of the men were away at the war, but since he had reached manhood he had stayed mostly around towns.

His mother, father and sister had uprooted themselves earlier that year and returned to the old country, England, there — presumably — to spend the rest of their days. Sam's decision to stay in America had disappointed his father and sister, and undermined his mother's health, but they had acknowledged his wishes and left him behind to make his own way in the world.

One thing they had given Sam, a good education. He could read well, and write passably good English prose. It was because of these comparatively rare skills that he took an interest in the newspapers of his time. In the past two or three years he had written for several, mostly those with famous names in towns like Fort Worth, Dallas, and Amarillo.

Cyprus P. Dingle, the owner and editor of the *Clarion* in Conchas City, had published his articles from time to time over a period of a year. After his parents had packed up and left, Sam decided to make the rounds of the papers which had published his work and, as a few dollars were owed to him by the proprietor of the *Clarion*, he had headed west into New Mexico first.

To his surprise, he had found the *Clarion* no longer functioning. Mr

Dingle had died and the newspaper, as a result, had folded up. Maggie Dingle, the widow, had a house on Second Street. She was a stooping woman in her middle sixties, short on energy and spending most of her time in the rocking chair on her front gallery.

She had been sympathetic to Sam when he visited her, telling him at once that she was low on funds, and giving him the keys to the office building so that he could look the place over. She had been quite agreeable to his using the place as an office for a time, and before he left she had intimated that if he could get the paper started up again she would be very pleased. Her words had acted as a challenge to him, but putting the paper on its feet again would not be easy. A young woman who helped Dingle had married and moved out, and a youth in his teens who had worked there had taken employment on a neighbouring ranch.

Sam emptied his glass and moved back to the bar to have it refilled. The barman was slow in coming to him, and he had time to study his reflection in the long mirror. His own green eyes looked back at him from under straight sun-bleached brows. In spite of the action of the sun and the freckles which liberally sprinkled the upper part of his face his complexion was still fresh. His reddish auburn hair was wavy, and combed straight back from his forehead. His sideburns were tapered to a point below his cheekbones. A dark green shirt and an even darker bandanna contrasted with his buttonless fawn vest.

His side-rolled dun stetson made his lean face look even longer when it was upon his head.

He collected his refill of beer, drank it quickly and left the saloon sucking on the first of his small cigars. He entered the *Clarion* office which was fifty yards away, and applied himself once again to the study of back numbers of the paper which he had discovered in a partitioned section where the records were kept.

The place smelled dusty and old; it needed an airing. Nevertheless, he applied himself once more to accounts of local happenings of a few years previously. One article in particular held his attention. It told how the young son of Judge H. Dan Sherman had lost his life in a canoeing accident near the spot on Pecos Creek known as Indian Rapids.

A few casual enquiries had elicited the information that the judge was something of a recluse. He had retired not far away, but no one wanted to say exactly where.

Sam took his lunch in a Chinese restaurant about one in the afternoon. It was his basic restlessness which prompted him to make an enquiry.

'How far is it to Pecos Creek, Chang?'

The oriental owner accentuated his wrinkles in a smile and blinked his slanting eyes. 'Two, maybe three miles west of here, I guess.'

'Say a fellow wanted a trip on the creek in a boat, maybe a canoe. How would he go about it?'

Chang paused with the stack of empty dishes easily perched on one hand. 'That's easy. Anyone so inclined would go lookin' for the shack of Methuselah, on a slope just north of the westbound trail. Methuselah ain't very active these days, but he does have one or two canoes.'

Sam thanked the Chinaman, paid him what was due and collected his black stallion from the last livery stable on the west end of Second Street. He left behind him a town which was already giving itself over to siesta in the hottest part of the day.

★ ★ ★

Two hours riding at a modest pace brought him to the isolated shack on the slope with Methuselah's name painted on a warped board nailed to the near side of the sloping roof.

Methuselah was sleeping noisily on the lower of two bunks with a half empty bottle of moonshine whisky on the floor beside him.

A crumpled notice on the home-made wooden table offered canoes for hire at one dollar a day, payable in advance. Methuselah's heavy snoring made it clear that he had no special interest in the business, and Sam decided to locate a canoe without assistance. There was a useful inlet a little further on. Drawn up on the bank were three canoes in an upturned position. Half a dozen paddles were grouped up like the supports for a tent between two trees.

Sam lit another cigar while he studied the boats for water-worthiness. He selected one with a wide beam, and after turning it over, slid it into the water. Next, he turned his attention to his mount. The black stallion was tossing its head and wondering about the next development. Should he leave it by the shack, or alongside of the creek?

This indecision prompted him to wonder how far he was prepared to go on the water, and how long he would be before he returned the boat. As it was difficult to come to a decision about the duration of the trip, he decided to slacken the black's saddle and allow it to wander by the water.

The black snickered its thanks as the tightness was eased. It plodded without haste towards the water, wrinkled its muzzle briefly over the surface and then drank. Meanwhile, Sam slipped into the canoe, hefted the paddle and cautiously eased his craft away from the bank.

Soon, he was in the main stream, gripped by the current and his attention was away from the bank. He coaxed the slim canoe into midstream and practised with the paddle. The motion was smooth and relaxing. On either bank, the levels rose and fell. Willows draped their leafy branches in the water, adding to the general soporific effect.

Sam pushed back his hat and started to think. Why had he come on this energetic trip so soon after reaching town and gaining access to the *Clarion*'s records? Had it been simply a desire for exercise of another kind, or had his 'nose' for a story made him want to look further into the tragedy of a year or so ago, when the judge's only son had lost his life? He supposed that it would be interesting to find out for himself whether the boy had been negligent in his handling of the canoe, or whether some other factor had contributed to his sad demise.

There had been times back in Amarillo when he had been called upon to act as an investigator. Sometimes he had received fees far in excess of the pay for his newspaper work. He could not help wondering if all the facts were known about the fatal accident.

Judge Herman, he knew, had once had a reputation as a crusader against wrong-doers. In particular he had investigated big crimes of fraud and the mounting activities of some of the bigger gangs of road agents which had infested the county where most of his court work had been done.

Maybe he would get to know the judge, in time. Perhaps a character like that might start off a series about great personalities in the area! He began to enthuse, and with his enthusiasm his stroke-making with the paddle became more effective.

A half hour passed quite quickly. In fact, he was surprised when he suddenly caught sight of a long painted board sticking out from under a bank-side tree warning canoers that the rapids were not far ahead. It was as well to heed the warning, as the locality was devoid of other humans.

At once, he checked the forward motion of the canoe, driving the paddle in deep first on one side and then on the other. A few cunning thrusts with the paddle sent him in close, on the same side where he had entered. For a few seconds, a low branch threatened to remove his hat, and then he was in with the knife bow nudging the soft soil of the bank and riding high.

All along the east bank he had open territory, or common land. As far as he could tell it was scarcely ever used by folks from the town. Maybe families picnicked on it from time to time, but that was all.

There had been no obstructions in the water during his trip which could foul up a canoe, although the muted angry roar not far ahead of him gave definite warning of dangerous rocks and speeding waters.

He used the tree branch to manoeuvre his light craft further inshore and scrambled up the bank. His short spell on water had been pleasant, but not altogether absorbing. He felt slightly cheated. No mystery had presented itself to him. In fact, other than the drunken Methuselah, whose memory was probably ruined by drink, he had met no one. No one with whom to converse about the tragedy of young Danny Sherman's death.

Sam squatted at the top of a short

slope in a thinker's pose; one prominent knee supporting an elbow, which in turn supported his chin. Surely there was someone in the region of the creek? He wondered about the other side which was some thirty or forty yards across the water.

Probably ranch land. Not much point in scrambling across it in the canoe because the cattle, cowpunchers and buildings were likely to be quite a distance from the creek. A pity he had left the black so far behind. But had he? He turned his head, stuck two fingers in his mouth and emitted a piercing whistle. At first there was no response, but the stallion had been carrying him for over a year and he knew the keenness of its ears. He had stretched out and his eyelids were growing heavy when the distant jingle of harness carried to him. He blinked, smiled and whistled again, this time without the use of his fingers.

The black trotted up shortly afterwards. Sam fondled its muzzle before partially tightening his saddle girth and swinging up into leather. As soon as he turned the muscular horse towards the water, it realised what was in store for them.

At the top of the slope, it moved its forefeet gingerly before stepping forward and launching itself into the creek with a powerful leap. Spray shot up in all directions. The white-blazed head momentarily disappeared under water before the powerful beast settled down and began to make progress across the current.

* * *

The peeled-log cabin of the elderly light-skinned negro Uncle Tim Paris and his brown-skinned wife, Nancy, was located some four hundred yards inland from the spot where Sam Gould urged his dripping mount ashore.

The building was in a secluded glade around which the trees in winter formed a wind-break. Although it only

14

had two rooms and a loft, the front of it was improved with a gallery which held a table, a rocking chair and two uprights.

At the time when Sam started his approach, Uncle Tim was lifting potatoes in the neat kitchen garden round the back. He was dressed in a white collarless shirt and baggy blue overalls. From time to time, his thick quiff of white hair slipped over his forehead. He pushed it back as he mopped his brow with his shirt sleeve. Nancy, a small gentle person in her late fifties, was in the house wringing out some clothes at the end of a week's wash. She it was who first saw Sam approaching on his horse.

At the time, she was emerging from the front door. A soiled white apron protected her long dark work dress. A wicker basket of wrung-out clothes hid her mild lined brown face and the black hair, streaked with white and parted down the middle.

'Good day to you, ma'am, is it all

right if I come over an' talk for a while?'

Nancy gasped in surprise, almost dropped her basket and then recovered with an effort. She lowered it onto the table of the gallery the better to be able to see the stranger. Her mute glance of enquiry was asking him where on earth he had come from, but her words were different.

'Glory be, young man, Uncle Tim an' me, we don't get many visitors tucked out here in the back of Box R ranchland! Why don't you dismount an' tell us what brought you here? I'll call my husband.'

Sam touched his hat, nodded and grinned and dismounted. He led the black slowly up to the rail in front of the gallery and tethered it. Uncle Tim came trotting round from the back, fastening metal-rimmed spectacles to his short-sighted eyes so as to see the visitor more clearly.

He said: 'Welcome, young fellow. Take a seat. Nancy'll make you some coffee an' bring you a slice of fruit pie if you smile at her real nice.'

Sam moved into one of the upright chairs while Uncle Tim cleaned his hands and Nancy spirited away the washing basket. In a very short time they were talking easily about everyday matters. Through the window, the visitor caught sight of a nicely-framed photograph of a stern-looking man with fierce eyes and a straight black moustache.

Sam, who had seen such a likeness before, had a question to ask.

'Sure enough, Sam, that's Judge Sherman himself. Like he was in the days when we kept house for him in town,' Uncle Tim explained.

'He was younger, then, you understand. That picture was taken when his wife was still around,' Nancy added. She nodded several times.

Sam pushed aside the plate which had held his fruit pie, and refused more coffee. 'I won't have anything else, Mrs Paris, but I thank you very kindly. Won't stay long, seein' as I'm on private ground belongin' to the Box R. I'd like to ask you both a question, though, before I get back across the creek.

'Some time before I ever thought of comin' into these parts, it seems the judge's young son, Danny, had a fatal accident while boatin' in a canoe . . . '

Sam's voice tailed off as he saw what his question was doing to his host and hostess. Nancy seemed to shrivel up, clutching at her dress over the bosom, while Uncle Tim's light brown complexion turned suddenly and ominously to off-grey. The old negro's mouth opened wide. His expression suggested a chest pain. He clawed his shirt front and gestured despairing towards his wife.

'Hold on, husband! Hold on!' Nancy called out, as she struggled to recover herself.

Sam was thinking to himself, Did I do *that* to them? He said: 'Tim's in trouble. His heart, ain't it? Tell me what to do an' I'll do it!'

Nancy recovered herself with an

effort. Following her instructions he went into the sitting room and came back with a small box of tablets which had been located on the shelf underneath the judge's portrait. Back on the gallery, she almost snatched them from him and produced one from the box, pushing it urgently between Tim's lips.

Sam held the old man steady while Nancy gave him lukewarm coffee to wash down the tablet. Gradually the stricken man's pains eased, and his colour returned. Sam backed off, feeling youthful, ignorant and ill-at-ease.

'I — I think something I said must have shocked you both. I'm sorry, very sorry. Whatever I said, I said without knowin' what it would do to you. How could I have known?'

Uncle Tim was looking past Sam into the trees beyond the house, but nothing in his eyes or his general expression suggested that he blamed the visitor for what happened. Nancy bathed her husband's face and brow with a moist cloth.

She murmured: 'We jest never talk about the accident to little Danny Sherman. As you say, you couldn't have known.'

Sam did a couple of jobs around the house, but from the time of the attack he felt ill-at-ease. He took his departure, making his way back to the creek, as soon as he could decently do so. His stunned brain was full of disquieting conjecture and foreboding for the future.

2

Uncle Tim's near heart attack had shaken Sam Gould more than anything he could remember. In his travels he had figured successfully in one or two brushes with trigger-happy westerners, but he had never seen a man stricken by a heart condition. The shock of what his words had done to the old negro sent him back to town in a very unsettled mood.

On his return to town, he had booked a room at the Conchas Hotel and given over the rest of the day to mooching about the place, weighing up the amenities, the saloons and the general attitude of the townsfolk towards strangers.

By shortly after eight o'clock the following morning, he was back in the newspaper office mulling over the old issues and trying to plan a future of sorts. Nothing happened to disturb him until almost nine o'clock. An unidentified noise in the street made him look up. He was in time to see a well-painted buckboard draw up with a spritely white-stockinged chestnut horse in the shafts and a smartly dressed, rather beautiful young woman holding the reins.

His pulse quickened in case she was coming into the office. He was disappointed. She merely fixed the brake and sat there as though waiting for someone. Her appearance, however, held his attention. He figured her for around twenty-one years of age. She had long sleek black hair shaped like a bell and turned in at the ends somewhere between her ears and shoulders.

A short fringe masked a broad forehead. Her wide-set blue eyes were matched by the broad band on a smart straw bonnet. She had on a pale blue blouse topped by a matching jacket and navy skirt which modestly accentuated her female shape. The hands clasped in her lap were hidden in white gloves which came up over her wrists. He found himself wondering if there were many more young women in the town to match this one for beauty. From time to time she glanced towards the office, but her interest was not marked.

Five minutes went by with Sam still not able to return to his reading because of the outside attraction. Just when he was wondering if he might stroll out of doors and speak to the girl, two men came along the sidewalk with a purposeful tread and brought his half-formed plans to an end.

The two men matched each other in height, being around six feet tall. The one with the marshal's badge was a lean cadaverous-looking fellow in his forties with a thin down-drooping black moustache not much thicker than the string tie at his throat. His black jacket was shiny. A black flat-topped hat with a straight brim made the long hair stand out over his ears and wide of his collar.

The other was heavier in build and a good twenty years older. He held himself erect like a man trained to military service. His fierce dark eyes struck Sam first. They were the same ones he had seen in the photograph at Uncle Tim's shack. Judge Sherman had aged a lot since his likeness had been taken. His cranial hair was grey now under the expensive cream stetson and his neatly-trimmed moustache was almost white. The jacket and trousers of his grey suit partially hid a small paunch which had developed since his retirement.

For a few seconds it seemed as if the girl on the buckboard would scramble down and join the two men, but the judge quickly dissuaded her and she stayed where she was, indicating her fleeting displeasure with a slight frown and a delicate shrugging of the shoulders.

Both men stared through the window

at Sam behind the desk. The marshal headed the judge into the room with an expression on his face which suggested hostility rather than friendship. Sam bounded to his feet with a broad ingenuous grin on his freckled face and indicated two upright chairs which he had dusted off earlier.

'Good day to you, gents. I believe I have the pleasure of addressin' Judge Sherman, and you must be the marshal of this town. Do take a seat. I wasn't expectin' visitors, but you're surely welcome.'

Sherman nodded curtly and sat down rather gingerly. The marshal, taking his cue from the judge, did the same.

'My name is Sam Gould. I'm new to Conchas City, as I'm sure you know. Mrs Dingle was kind enough to give me the run of the old *Clarion* building. Er, what can I do for you?'

Sherman gave the marshal a sharp look, which prompted him to speak. 'Pete Stevens, marshal of this here

25

town, as you guessed. Word has come to my office that you were trespassin' on ranch property yesterday. To be exact, on the property of Lincoln Roder, who owns the Box R. I have to warn you that if you trespass again action will be taken against you.'

Stevens was ill at ease. He brushed the drooping ends of his moustache, cleared his throat and glanced sideways to see whether the judge wanted to take up the conversation.

Sam kept his voice on a calm, everyday tone. 'All right, marshal, I'll take heed of your warnin', although I didn't do any harm in my short spell on ranch land.' He suddenly remembered Uncle Tim's sad condition and that made him add: 'At least no harm was intended. But I'm sure you didn't need to bring along a retired circuit judge to back up your words. I'm used to keepin' to the law.'

Sam turned his attention rather pointedly to the judge, and Marshal Stevens remained silent.

Sherman spoke in a low voice, which carried easily. 'Is it your intention to start up this newspaper again, young man?'

Sam beamed. 'It is indeed. This is the opportunity of a lifetime for a man with my special interests! I've had a lot of practice in writin' pieces for newspapers, an' Mrs Dingle I believe would dearly like to see her husband's paper on its feet again.'

Sherman yawned rather delicately behind his hand, while Sam stole a glance at the girl waiting outside. It had just occurred to him that she was probably the judge's daughter.

'We know a whole lot about your journalistic efforts, young fellow, an' your attempts to work as an investigator. No doubt you feel you can't do any harm with Mrs Dingle's backin' an' all, but a lot of thinkin' people in this town believe the *Clarion* ought not to be started up again. The widow's friends will see she comes to no harm.'

Sam's open face mirrored his surprise. 'I think you must have good reason for comin' along to tell me this sort of news, judge. I can't say I ever expected a man of your callin' wantin' the press muzzled. Why, it's one of the everyday freedoms of ordinary folks in the United States — the freedom of the press, no less.'

The expression on the judge's lined face hardened. 'If you do go ahead in your intention to get this newspaper printed again, be so kind as to leave all mention of my family out of it. That goes for me, too. If you must dabble, make up things out of your head like most western editors do. A bit of fiction in the articles never did anyone any harm.'

Sam blinked and finger-combed his hair. 'If you are still sensitive about the unfortunate accident to your son, judge, I can understand that. But I must have freedom to say what I like in print!'

'I *am* sensitive about my son's death, an' so are a lot of other people in this area, Gould. An' what's more I've changed my mind. I'm tellin' you to write things an' send them elsewhere. Let the *Clarion* go on sleepin'! You look like a bullheaded redhead to me who doesn't know good advice when he hears it, so I'm warnin' you not to print the paper. An' that's all, I guess, so we'll be goin'.'

Sherman rose abruptly, Stevens more slowly. In the doorway, the marshal turned, as though he had to underline the judge's words.

'Gould, you must understand that the prominent citizens of Conchas have a right to say whether they want a newspaper or not! It's a local matter for the folks who've spent their lives here. You've heard the judge's rulin'. Mind you heed it.'

Sam almost choked on a touch of temper. 'A judge in retirement doesn't make rules, marshal, as you ought to know. I don't like what lies behind this interview an' I'm not givin' any sort of undertakin' about my future intentions. Good day to you!'

The two men withdrew. Sam pretended to bury himself in the papers before him on the desk, but he was so angry he could not see the print. Outside, the two men stood talking in whispers beside the buckboard while the personable young woman frowned at what she overheard. Eventually, the pair parted. Marshal Stevens strode off down the sidewalk, while Judge Sherman climbed up beside his daughter. The two Shermans glared in at the window before the judge kicked off the brake, tugged on the reins and started the buckboard in motion.

Sam sagged back in his chair, put his hands behind his head and whistled. In twenty-four hours he seemed to have made two formidable enemies. With his eyes half-closed, he ran his thoughts back over what he had known previously of Sherman's reputation, backed up by what he had read in the files.

The judge obviously felt very strongly about the paper re-appearing, but what sort of notions could have put him — of all people — in that frame of mind? The mystery baffled Sam. He had doubts as to whether any of the old issues would enlighten him as to what he was up against. Maybe there was more to the son's demise than met the eye. Perhaps the judge had a skeleton or two in his family cupboard.

Unfortunately for Sam, his bump of curiosity was an outsize one. He doubted if he could stop himself from going forward with his project, even if events shaped up to make things difficult.

For a time, he gave way to his restlessness. He left the office and went up the street to take coffee. He was disappointed that the judge's comely daughter was no longer in sight.

Later that morning, he unearthed several articles of a general nature which had never been published. Pieces of interest to westerners which time did not date. The discovery of them made him even more angry about his earlier advice to leave the *Clarion* be.

In the afternoon, he went back to the time around the Sherman boy's death. From there, he turned back a few weeks and made another discovery. Many copies were missing. It was as if they had been deliberately removed, because old Cyrus P. Dingle had been meticulous in detail, even in his declining years.

One single paper for that era turned up in the wrong heap. Sam pulled it out lovingly and dusted it off, willing it to tell him something of the mystery he was only guessing about.

There was one wordy lead article about three notorious gangs in Conchas and surrounding counties. Judge Herman Dan Sherman was quoted on two or three occasions. The editor was saying that the judge held evidence that there was a connection between the activities of the vastly differing outlaw gangs. In fact, the learned man was suggesting that the brains behind all three was the same unknown sinister figure.

In another part of the paper the

judge had allowed his name to be used in an advertisement for the celebrated Pinkerton detective agency. Sam wondered if there was a tie-up between the judge's 'evidence' regarding the control of outlaw gangs and a thriving office of the great detective agency not too far away.

He went for a swim in the nearest part of the creek late that afternoon and resumed his reading in his hotel room after the evening meal. His mind was unusually active as the light faded. Unfortunately, he was unable to sleep. After an hour in total darkness, long after midnight, he rose from his comfortable single bed, lit a lamp and played a lone hand at chess, using a travelling set he had found in a cupboard.

Even the chess did not calm him. The black and white squares were running into one another when he gave up, dressed himself and went out for a walk along the boards. Inevitably, he walked towards the *Clarion* office, his nostrils

33

dilating at the thought of printer's ink. He paused uncertainly in the doorway, tried the handle and found it unlocked. This surprised him, as he had been very careful to lock the door before coming away.

Nothing seemed amiss, but he stuck his head inside and the first thing he noticed was the smell of lamp oil and a wick which had been burning. He had not lit the lamp himself, and this phenomenon drew him inside. The desk and its contents were intact. He lit and carried his lamp through the flimsy partition which separated the office from the printing machinery and there a disturbing sight met his eyes.

The drawers of type had been removed. Someone had smashed the rollers and two drive wheels. A very workmanlike job had been done, one which must have needed some strength and caused a lot of noise for a short time.

Even as the anger bubbled up inside of him, he knew that the *Clarion* was likely to remain a dead newspaper after this. He wasn't going to be given a chance to start it up again. Someone, and he thought he knew who, was determined to go to any lengths to prevent its re-creation.

This far, he had not visited the marshal's office on Main Street, but now he searched it out, using the flickering illumination of the occasional lamps still lighting the sidewalk. He threw open the door without ceremony, but his anger ebbed when he saw that only an ancient constable occupied a cot in an open cell. The old man's liquid supper — what remained of it — was in a bottle on the floor beside him, along with a battered ear trumpet.

Sam withdrew, shaking a window in its frame as he closed the door.

3

By ten o'clock the following morning, Sam Gould had worked off a whole lot of nervous energy in anger and frustration, and he still had to find a sympathetic soul to listen to him. He walked the whole length of Main Street down one sidewalk and came back down the other.

A family of shoppers going the other way made him pause under the shingle of one Walter Vilman, the town lawyer. He studied the name, hesitated, took off his hat and scratched his head, a habit he had when uncertain what to do.

Acting on impulse, he pushed open the door and was confronted by a middle-aged bespectacled clerk in the front office.

'Good day to you, stranger. Something we can do for you?'

'Sure. My name's Sam Gould. I'm new in town. I'd like to talk to Mr Vilman, on business.'

'I'll see if he can spare you the time, Mr Gould.'

The clerk went through a frosted glass door into the rear office, and returned without haste two or three minutes later. He announced that Mr Vilman would see Sam, and stood aside for him to go through.

Vilman was seated behind a leather-topped desk writing on some sort of official paper. He glanced up, indicated the client's upright chair in front of the desk and went on writing. Sam removed his hat, hung it on a hickory hat stand and took the chair. Vilman finished his writing, pushed aside his work and made a steeple with the fingers of his two hands. He was a slim, dark, dapper man in his middle forties. His thinning black hair was greased, parted and slicked down to his head with hair oil. He had light bags under his grey eyes, a thin mouth and a pointed chin. The chain of a gold hunter linked the pockets of a fawn vest under his dark business jacket.

'What can I do for you, Mr Gould? You look like a man with a problem.'

In spite of himself, Sam managed to grin. 'I've had nothing but problems since I hit this burg, Mr Vilman. Perhaps I ought to outline them. A man in your profession ought to appreciate my kind of troubles.

'First off, Mrs Dingle said for me to use the *Clarion* office, seein' as how I'm used to writing an' her late husband owes me money. I wanted to get the paper on its feet again, an' she was agreeable. That's where my troubles started. Judge Sherman came along with the marshal and between them they tried to talk me out of it.

'I got the impression the judge was mighty keen to keep his private affairs private. I guess I must have rubbed him up the wrong way, because before he left he warned me to leave off exhumin' the paper. Me, I'm not easily put off. I told him he was infringin' the freedom of the press, an' he didn't like that.'

On the other side of the desk, Vilman's nervous fingers were doing a double tattoo like the legs of a spider in difficulties. At the same time, a ghost of a smile played around the corners of the lawyer's thin lips.

'Go ahead,' Vilman prompted.

'Durin' last night, a person or persons unknown broke into the *Clarion* office an' wrecked the machinery beyond repair. That's what I'm so riled up about. I informed the marshal early this morning. He took the matter quite calmly. In fact, too calmly. He didn't show any enthusiasm for findin' the culprits, an' for my money I don't think he means to make an arrest. He might even know who did it! So where does that leave me, an' Mrs Dingle, for that matter?'

Vilman cleared his throat. 'A difficult situation, I do admit, Mr Gould, you bein' a stranger in these parts an' all. I can pacify you on one point, though.

Old Cyrus Dingle had a lot of friends in this town. I mean if the widow ran short of funds she would be taken care of.

'As for you an' your ambition to start up the newspaper, that's more difficult. Without actually wantin' to, you may have created enemies in town. I don't think you're goin' to make a whole lot of progress here, at least, not in the near future. You see, it's no good goin' around hintin' that the marshal may be implicated in what has happened, nor anyone else for that matter.

'My advice to you is play it cool for a while. Or, move out an' seek a pitch some place else.'

Sam sighed and shrugged. 'Mr Vilman, I've travelled a long way to make personal contact with Dingle. I don't like movin' on again without havin' achieved anything. Er, when I'm not seekin' work for the papers I sometimes take on investigations. I don't suppose you could push any of that sort of work my way?'

Vilman slowly raised his brows, and smiled broadly for the first time. 'Well, if you're prepared to leave town for a while, there is a little job I could put your way. Jest recently, a man came through here, signed in at the hotel as John Brodie. We've since discovered there's a reward out for him as a confidence trickster under the name of John 'Ringo' Brocius. Makes his own bills, mostly of one hundred dollars. He paid a gamblin' debt with one. Someone spilled some beer on it after he'd left, and the inks smeared.

'If you'd like to go after him as far as Bridgetown, where he almost certainly is, you might take him there an' win yourself five hundred dollars reward. I can offer you a retainer of fifty dollars to tide you over for a few days. What do you say?'

Sam beamed. His immediate frustrations seemed to be suddenly minimised. Even if Vilman was only doing this to get him out of town temporarily, it was still an interesting proposition.

'I say, yes, siree, Mr Vilman. How far is Bridgetown, an' what other details can you tell me about the villain?'

Vilman grinned broadly again, showing tobacco stained teeth.

'Bridgetown is some fifteen miles to the north. Of course, we could telegraph the town, but we would still have to catch him passin' his home-made money, or catch him with the notes on him. I'm glad you've decided to take the job. It would be a good mark against your name if you were instrumental in havin' this parasite put away.'

Vilman talked for another ten minutes before handing over the retainer and showing his client out.

★ ★ ★

When he had a specific job to do, Sam was a very determined character. He spared neither himself nor others. He drove his black hard towards the north for many hours, pulled up when he was in danger of sapping his mount's stamina and slept out of doors.

He was a dusty sweat-stained character when he rode up the central thoroughfare of the town known as Bridgetown in the hour before midday. The black was wilting and Sam was badly in need of some liquid nourishment to recoup his dehydrating body, but he put aside the needs of himself and the horse in the interests of his job.

A flapping painted canvas awning hung down from the first floor of the Robert E. Lee Hotel on the north side, and Sam turned his mount towards it. Stacked along the boards and in the entrance to the hotel were many carpet bags and leather valises. Enough to suggest that several visitors were on the point of departure by coach.

Sam began to have a feeling that his luck might be in. He hitched his mount to railings near a trough a little further along, and backtracked on foot to speak with the pear-shaped male clerk who was hovering about under the awning looking important. A green eyeshield hid the clerk's eyes and an apron of the same colour accentuated his prominent paunch.

'Pardon me, but I'm lookin' for a friend. Do you have a Mr John Brodie stayin' with you at this moment?'

The clerk put up his eyeshield and squinted short-sightedly into Sam's face. 'Well, we're the only hotel in town worth callin' a hotel, but I do have a bad memory for names. Lemme see . . . '

Sam leaned against an upright, mopping himself with his green bandanna, which needed a scrub. 'My friend is a small, jovial sort of fellow with a bald head. He has thick greying side whiskers an' goes in for bright waistcoats . . . '

Sam went on with his description. In his excitement, he had raised his voice higher than usual. Unknown to him, it carried to an open window on the first floor above the awning. Somebody puffed cigar smoke out of the window and leaned closer to listen.

Presently, the clerk slapped his chest. 'Why, I know who you're talkin' about! That's Mr Brocius. He paid his bill not long ago. Used room No 16 on the first floor. Mr *Brocius*, not Brodie, stranger. He'll be takin' the stage east in a half hour with the other folks.' The clerk sniffed, without making it too personal. 'You'll have time to cool yourself down a piece, take on some beer if you need it, an' then catch him before he quits town. He could be in the saloon, himself — '

The clerk would have said more, but Sam cut him short with a pat on the back and a word of thanks. 'I'll take your advice, an' thanks. By the way, you don't happen to know if he paid his bill with a hundred dollar note, do you?'

Sam was some yards away by now, and the clerk did not hear any too well. 'How's that again?'

'It doesn't matter,' Sam called back. 'Thanks again!'

He moved into the saloon two

buildings away, sniffed the atmosphere and lengthened his stride towards the bar.

★ ★ ★

Meanwhile, the small crafty character known sometimes as Brodie and at other times as Brocius, quaked. He tip-toed down the back staircase of the hotel, went out at the back and crossed over two or three vacant lots until he was in the alley on the far side of the saloon. The tip of his tongue was busy, constantly moistening his dry lips. He had heard enough to know that someone fresh into town was hot on his trail and knew his principle means of livelihood.

At the street end of the alley, he paused and rested against a wall with his heart thumping. His small restless eyes were busy in both directions. His bags. He could not leave without his bags . . .

Presently, a young boy in cut down

pants came back from a wagon which had gone through and made a short stop further down the street. The boy slowed with a silver dollar in his hand. His anxious eyes met those of the equally anxious skulking counterfeiter, who made himself smile and crooked a finger in the lad's direction.

'Mister, would you go in the saloon an' get me a bottle of whisky? My Pa's in a hurry an' sometimes the barmen won't serve me with a bottle on account of my age.'

'Keep your dollar. I'll make a bargain with you. There's a bottle of whisky in my valise. All you have to do to get it for free is fetch my gear from in front of the hotel. Take it along to your Pa an' ask him to give me a short lift out of town towards the east. Think you can do that?'

'Oh, sure, sure, mister. Pa'll be glad to give you a lift. He says we've got too many women with Ma an' my sisters!'

Brodie grabbed him, hoping that youthful excitement would not foul up his plan. 'Look for the initials, 'J.B.' on one carpet bag an' one leather holdall. Understand? Don't make a lot of fuss. I have my reasons. I'll join your Pa jest clear of town. Got it?'

'Sure, sure, I understand, mister. You don't have to sweat on it. Take your time. Pa'll wait.'

The youngster went off. He was efficient. Ten minutes later, Brodie was concealed in the back of the wagon, heading east. Later, still, he transferred his bags and his body to the stagecoach when it overtook them.

★ ★ ★

Sam came on the alert again when the passengers started to assemble to board the stagecoach. He chatted with the driver, spoke again with the hotel clerk and only began to think there was something wrong when Brodie failed to turn up. He, himself, pointed out that there did not appear to be any baggage for his 'friend' and when he accompanied the clerk to No 16 and found it bare he knew that the counterfeiter had slipped away. His intention had been to confront the forger with his wrong-doings and hope that he would break down and confess.

Now, he knew the odds were against success. He mounted his horse, did a quick tour of the town and failed to come up with any clues. Fifteen minutes later, he was back again and, as the clerk seemed to be away from his counter, he went back to the front room and began a minute search of the furniture.

He had almost given up when he mounted a chair and saw something which set his pulses racing on top of a large wall cupboard which served as a wardrobe. It was a flat leather pouch. He moved the chair to the wardrobe and looked on the top. Laid out, apparently to dry, were no fewer than twenty one hundred dollar bills.

At least he would have something to

show lawyer Vilman when he returned to Conchas City. After that, he made the acquaintance of the hotel manager, showed a briefing letter which the lawyer had provided and left the matter of telegraphing the local towns to the Bridgetown authorities.

After sluicing himself down under a pump, having the black groomed and fed, he took a meal and left town again at a more leisurely pace. Bridgetown was to the north-west of Conchas, rather than the north, as Vilman had intimated.

It was four in the afternoon when he rode out again. The pull of water always drew him and he determined to go back making a slight detour so that he could bathe in the creek which ran west of Conchas. That night he camped beside the remote waterway and swam for a half hour before turning in. In the morning, he tried his hand at fishing, but all he managed to catch were two small fish which he tossed back again. In spite of the setback to his pride, the bacon and beans went down well.

He took another bathe before mounting up and continuing his journey. All about the east side of the creek the terrain was natural and unbroken by trails. Seas of mesquite and sage abounded in huge patches, broken at times with large areas of fern and bunch grass. For two hours, he circled the scrub, dawdled over the lush grass and otherwise headed from one stunted tree stand to the next.

The distance between himself and the creek gradually widened as he maintained a south-easterly direction. To westward and the north, high peaks of the southern Rockies hung in a cloudless sky above the nearer foothills. Everything seemed remote: earthly problems included.

It took an effort to bring the mind back to the immediate past and Sam was trying to figure out how far he was north of Methuselah's shack when the unexpected happened once again. Right there in the shadow of a big stunted oak was a horse. A big-boned dun with a black mane and tail, saddled and sweat-stained, cropping the grass with no signs of its owner.

The redheaded young man should have been warned at the outset, but all he felt for a few moments was curiosity. The black showed an interest, too. In the last fifty yards the young rider made a surprising discovery. The dun was lame in its left forefoot. It straightened its neck and tossed its mane as they pulled up a few yards away.

Even then the redhead's curiosity was fully centred upon the horse. His mind had not turned to the missing rider. He bent and lifted the left forefoot to see if a stone was lodged in the shoe.

'Hold it right there, stranger!'

Sam froze in his crouch, merely turning his head to look over his shoulder in the direction of the menacing voice. It came from a tall man in a suit of fringed buck-skin who had materialised from behind the tree bole. A long-barrelled Colt held in a gloved hand was pointing directly at Sam's back.

'Hold on yourself, stranger,' Sam protested. 'I didn't aim to *steal* your horse. I was only checkin' it for a stone in the shoe!'

'Toss your revolver aside an' stand up, real slow. That's my boy. The old dun has sprained a tendon. You look as if you're mighty keen on hoss flesh an' that's good, because I aim to take your stallion an' leave my bronc with you.'

Sam coloured up behind his tan and his freckles. 'Jest like that, you aim to steal my horse. Right out here, miles away from anywhere. You must have done something real bad.'

Under the battered flat-crowned stetson, the stranger wore his very fair hair almost down to his collar. A yellow bandanna carelessly pulled up over the lower part of his face scarcely masked the stubbled chin. The man with the gun chuckled without humour.

'The law is what a man cares to make it out in the wilds, amigo, so don't go rilin' me up. I could put a bullet in you an' take everything you've got. As it is, I propose to make sure you don't follow me, an' merely swop mounts. Get over by that tree, pronto.'

In a matter of minutes Sam was secured to the tree in a standing position. He managed to keep himself under control and held his tongue until the trussing with the lariat was almost complete. Then, rather belatedly, he spoke up. His assailant slapped him hard across the face and while his head was still singing through contact with the tree bole, his bandanna was tightly fixed across his mouth.

In that vastly uncomfortable position, he could only breath through his nose. Hatless, he blinked salt perspiration out of his eyes as he was forced to watch his ambusher mount up on the black and take the direction he had just come from.

4

The task of freeing himself taxed Sam's patience to the limit. At first, he had to work hard to control his temper and regularise his breathing. After that, it was a matter of tortuous wriggling and muscle control.

The loop of the lariat holding his neck close to the tree bole troubled him a lot as he contrived to slide the lower loops off his chest and down his abdomen. After working hard for upwards of fifteen minutes he managed to free one leg. Next, he freed the second leg.

As soon as his lower limbs were free, he had sufficient slack to gradually slip his neck out of the offending noose, although his skin suffered in patches before his head was released. He worked with his teeth to undo the knots round one wrist. The other was quickly loosened and only then was he able to sag into a sitting position against the trunk and massage his sore mouth where the bandanna had cut into it.

The loss of his horse, his saddle and the Winchester which he always had with him made him feel depressed. It was several more minutes before he admitted to himself that things could have been worse. His attacker, a desperate man, might easily have killed him and moved on without anyone being the wiser.

He found water in the canteen hanging from the dun's saddle. That helped a little. The Henry rifle in the scabbard was a poor exchange for his Winchester. A brief examination of the dun showed a swelling above the fetlock in the left foreleg. As he did not feel like walking all the way to Methuselah's shack, he tore a strip off the bottom of his shirt and used it to strap up the weak limb. At the same time, he reminded himself that the leather pouch was still at his back, inside the shirt, above his belt. He still had the counterfeiter's bills to the value of two thousand dollars.

The ambush setback had dampened his ardour for further saddle travel, but nothing was to be gained by prolonging his journey. He paced around for a few minutes to take the stiffness out of his limbs, then mounted up and started off again with the dun maintaining a slow painful walk.

Conchas City was still several miles away. He wondered whether he could ease his problems by visiting Methuselah's shack again, as it was considerably nearer.

He was still not sure what he should do when a bunch of horsemen, all riding hard, began to approach him from a southerly direction. The riders were about ten in number. A man with a deputy sheriff's badge forged ahead of the others and came up alongside of him in a spectacular stop.

A revolver was pointed at him from a distance of five yards.

'Drop your gun, an' raise your hands!'

Before Sam had any time to react, the rest of the riders had ringed him round. This was the second time in a short period of hours that a gun had been pointed at him. A streak of stubbornness prevented him from complying. He swung slowly out of leather on the same side as the deputy and folded his arms.

'My name is Sam Gould. I'm returnin' to Conchas City after doin' a job out of town for Mr Vilman, the lawyer. What can I do for you?'

'We're huntin' a killer, Gould, so don't go takin' any liberties with me. Can you prove who you are?'

'I'm known to the judge, Marshal Stevens an' the lawyer, but I can't prove that unless I'm allowed to proceed to Conchas. Right now, I'm in a funny mood, too. I've jest been jumped by a man in a buckskin suit who tied me to a tree an' made off with my horse, a black stallion. This one he left for me is lame.'

As soon as his words where heard, the deputised riders broke out in excited conjecture among themselves.

'Sounds like the man we're lookin' for. Which way did he go?'

Sam was a few seconds in answering. He was studying the appearance of his questioner. The deputy was very tall and lean, in his middle thirties. He was cleanshaven. His brown hair was cut short under an undented stetson. The badge was pinned to a bright checked shirt. A white bandanna encircled a long thin neck, hanging down in front over a hirsute chest.

'He went off towards the north. Now, how far is it to Methuselah's shack?'

No one listened to the request for information. The deputy, whose name was Rex Hollis, was eager to get moving again and catch the fugitive before he had the chance to elude the posse. Abruptly, the ring of horses broke up. Sam was left with his arms folded, coughing on their dust. He cupped his hands to his face and shouted after them.

'Which way to Methuselah's?'

One of the rearmost riders paused long enough to point in the direction from which they had appeared. In less than a minute, only dust, a turmoil of horsehoe prints and a rapidly fading sound of hard-ridden horses remained to mark Sam's second encounter of the day. As he mounted up, new thoughts were pushing his frustrations into the back of his mind. No one had thought to tell him who had been killed. Was it someone in town, or a man in an isolated place, like Methuselah himself?

He decided to make for Methuselah's shack, in any case.

The ride on the limping horse took fifteen minutes. As he came up to the building, the old bewhiskered prospector was in the act of tipping a bucket of water over his head, standing beside a well at the rear of the building.

Methuselah sucked in air through his mouth which was a small red aperture entirely surrounded by grey facial hair.

His crown was bald. The upper part of his overall fitted his fleshy chest like a blue skin, being soaked with water.

Sam nodded to him, dismounted and ambled into the shack where he was brought up short by the barrel-chested corpse of a man in his middle fifties stretched out upon a worn blanket. The dead man had been shot in the chest from close range. Blood stained the upper half of his frockcoat and a shirt which had been white. A flat Quaker-style hat lay on the blanket.

Sam whistled as he recognized the lined weather-beaten face.

He said: 'Walter V. Grout, God rest his soul.'

Methuselah walked in behind him. 'I take it that you know him, stranger? Used to work for the Pinkerton detective agency, by all accounts. Reckon he was comin' to see me. Can't think why, though. Can't say as I've ever met him before.'

'Was he killed right here?'

'Nope. It happened in the trees no

more than fifty yards away. I was sleepin' at the time. Never did get to see the killer's face.'

Sam seated himself on an upright chair. 'Sure, I knew Walter Grout. I helped him with a surveillance job once back in Fort Worth. Never thought he's come to this sort of end, though. The man who jumped me an' took my horse must have been the one who shot him.'

Methuselah put the coffee pot on the stove. He mooched about, coughed as though he had a wheezy chest, and murmured something about the undertaker coming out from town to collect the body.

Sam mused: 'I wonder why he was killed? Must have been a case of personal enmity, or else it was done to stop him speakin' to somebody. If you never knew him, who could that be?'

The old man muttered to himself, but apparently any sort of an answer was beyond his fuddled brain. He walked outside as though to take care of some chore or another. Sam helped himself to the coffee as soon as it boiled. By the time he had drunk it, the town undertaker had arrived on a buckboard.

Slim Travis's appearance belied his nickname. He was fiftyish and fat, a bulky taciturn individual in a black suit and a stove-pipe hat. Sam tried twice to engage him in conversation about the dead man, failed to evoke any interest and promptly gave up, leaving the new-comer to drink all that remained in the coffee pot and help himself to biscuits.

Suddenly, Sam felt the need to get back into town. The day had produced more than a reasonable quota of surprises. He wandered out of doors, contacted Methuselah who was half-heartedly grooming the dead man's horse, a buckskin and intimated that he intended to borrow it for the rest of his ride into town.

The old man turned it over to him as if he had a perfect right to use it, and soon he was on his way, riding the buckskin and leading the lame dun.

The afternoon was well advanced when he reached town. He found himself possessed by a gnawing hunger and a thirst which would take a lot of beer to slake. Mindful of his mission, however, he walked both horses to the law office and reported to Walter Vilman about his efforts in Bridgetown.

The lawyer seemed impressed with the counterfeit notes which he handed over, even though he had been outwitted by the forger. Vilman exchanged a few ideas about the death of Grout, the former Pinkerton detective, without specifically naming anyone the detective might have been trying to contact.

To cut the interview short, the lawyer stood up and shook hands with Sam. 'I didn't expect you back this soon, an' you did reasonably well on the job I gave you. Keep the balance of the retainer for your efforts. Anythin' else I can do for you this trip?'

'Thanks. Yes, there is, Mr Vilman. Tell me if the town marshal has located the jasper who smashed up the *Clarion* printin' press.'

Vilman seemed surprised. He slipped his hunter watch into his waistcoat pocket and absently fingered his chin. 'Why, no, I don't believe he has. If I were you I'd forget about the whole incident. Take the judge's advice. Turn your mind to other things. There could be a place here in Conchas City for you, if you don't rub people up the wrong way.'

A blunt reply came to the redhead's lips, but remained unuttered. Sam nodded, smiled, and walked out into the street. He visited the livery, turned in both horses and recommended the dun for treatment. After that, he cleaned himself, drank modestly of beer, and ate quite a substantial meal in the Chinaman's cafe.

On his way up the stairs to his room at the Conchas Hotel, an interesting idea struck him. What if the ex-detective had been on his way to contact Judge Sherman? There was no indication at all that Grout had been seeking the judge, and yet it was an interesting notion.

He was still mulling over the events of the day when he fell asleep on his bed.

5

The disturbing news of the stranger's demise near Methuselah's cabin soon spread around that part of the county. Men were discussing the bizarre happening long before Sam Gould turned in that night.

To most of the townsfolk, the dead man was just a stranger, but there were those who knew him and what his main job in life had been. Between nine and ten o'clock the following morning, Judge Sherman made the long ride into town from his remote house on the Box R ranch home of the man referred to earlier as Lincoln Roder.

As soon as he arrived, the judge went off the street and took light refreshment in the dining room of the Conchas Hotel. While he sipped his coffee, a messenger made the rounds of two or three places making the judge's wants known.

At ten o'clock precisely, Sherman, Town Marshal Pete Stevens and Walter Vilman went into conference in the private office of the latter. All three smoked and the expressions on their faces showed that they were considerably ill-at-ease.

At length, Sherman knocked an inch of cigar ash off the cheroot he was smoking and opened up the conversation.

'Well, friends, I don't need to spell out to you what W. V. Grout's appearance in the area has done to my morale. Especially since he has been murdered before he could make contact with me and say what it was he had in mind.

'His appearance in this area could only have meant an emergency of some sort. It's my belief my old enemies are likely to go on the rampage again. Grout was comin' to bring a warnin' of some sort. I wonder what it was?'

Stevens said: 'I sure as hell hope things ain't as bad as we're thinkin' but I figure we have to prepare for the worst. Maybe one of the senior members of the gangs we helped to break up is due out of the penitentiary.'

Vilman also tried to calm the troubled judge, but he, too, was in a gloomy mood. He passed over a sheet of telegraph office pad. On it was a one sentence message. The letters of the words did not make any sense. Only the initials at the end made any sense. 'WVG.'

Vilman pointed to them with his forefinger.

'This message came through from Butte, further south, about two days ago. I didn't bother to inform you about it, judge, seein' as how it didn't make sense. At the time, I didn't know the significance of the initials. Now, of course, they seem to stand for Walter V. Grout, the murdered man.'

The judge discarded his cream stetson and placed a pair of reading glasses on his nose. He soon frowned at his disability to decipher the message and impatiently turned it over to

Stevens, who had even less ability over puzzles.

'There's a message there, of sorts,' Sherman opined. 'Pity we don't know the code Grout was usin'.' He had no confidence in the marshal's being able to read the message. Consequently, he went on talking. 'Be frank with me, you two. What am I goin' to do?'

Vilman tapped a pencil on his teeth. 'Frankly, judge, if the VIP we suspected before is goin' to try an' get at you again for what you achieved earlier in the break-up of the three gangs, I don't think you can sidestep the issue.

'Either you head for the coast an' take a long boat trip with Melissa, or you take every precaution for her safety and yours. And you do what you can to keep track of any unwanted developments.'

The marshal slipped the coded message back onto the desk, shaking his head.

'Even at *my* age, an' after what happened to my boy, I don't relish goin' on a world cruise jest to stay out of trouble. How can I keep track of unwanted developments, Walter?'

'Like you did in the past. Employ an investigator. One not known to be associated with us in any way.'

The judge's fierce dark eyes narrowed in concentration for a few seconds, and then his face cleared. 'You mean that young fellow who wanted to open up the newspaper again. Sam Gould. I wonder if he'd be any good?'

Talking straight at the judge, Vilman murmured: 'I sent him after that counterfeiter to Bridgetown, an' he all but caught him. Besides, he's young an' keen, an' he actually met the jasper who killed Grout. Why not send him after the killer, who has almost certainly gone in the direction of West Flats?'

West Flats was a settlement across a loop on Pecos Creek, located due west of Bridgetown. The judge nodded slowly. 'We'd have to tell him most of the truth about what happened to my boy. Maybe it *is* a good idea to sign him on. Why don't we have him over here, right away?'

Retirement had not dimmed the judge's brain. He could still make up his mind almost instantly.

* * *

Sam joined them twenty minutes later. He was surprised when each of the three men in turn stood up and shook him by the hand. Vilman pushed a glass of whisky towards him, while the judge plied him with one of his own cheroots and provided him with a light. Sam was at once aware that the initial hostility towards him had gone.

'Sit down, Sam,' Vilman invited.

When they had all resumed their seats, Sherman opened up the conversation. 'The last time we met, young man, I was very brusque with you, certain things I'm goin' to reveal to you now will, I hope, make you understand why Stevens and I acted the way we did.'

Staring at the wall opposite, Sherman

put words to things he had hoped never to discuss again. 'The death of my son was no accident. Certain investigations carried out in my name led to the break up of three gangs, men who had been terrorizin' a big area of this territory.

'The Red River gang, the Mavericks and the Holzer outfit. Some of them were killed durin' raids on banks and other anti-social happenings. Others went to the territorial penitentiary. But we never did nail the brains behind the three outfits. He remained in the background.

'And that wasn't all. My boy, Danny, was kidnapped. In order to have him released I had to pay five thousand dollars and surrender a dossier of information built up on the gangs over a long period. Even then we were not sure of the top man's identity, but we guessed that he was a man with a deal of power connected to at least one man near to the territorial governor.

'Anyway, we parted with the information an' the money. Danny was put into a canoe not far from the spot where Methuselah has his cabin. What we didn't know as we waited out of sight on the other bank of the creek was that he was heavily trussed and his body weighted. Furthermore, the underside of the canoe was gashed so that it would fill with water. To cut a long story short, the canoe became water-logged and the boy was drowned.'

Towards the end of that last sentence, the judge's voice faded almost to a whisper. He seemed reluctant to go on.

Sam murmured: 'I am very sorry to hear of your trouble, an' I regret havin' brought the matter into the open again. Clearly, my actions were ill advised. But, er, am I right in thinkin' there's been some new development, now that you've decided to tell me all this?'

Vilman cleared his throat. 'You're on the right lines, Sam. Grout came into this area to warn the judge of something or another. You saw his killer, an' we want you to work on the judge's behalf because we believe the unknown man or men who eliminated the boy may be takin' it upon themselves to have a go at the judge, himself, or his daughter.'

'You'd have to work on your own, Sam,' the marshal pointed out. 'We can give you one or two clues where to start lookin', an' there's a peculiar cryptic message on a telegraph pad hereabouts. My belief is that Grout sent it ahead of himself to warn us. It's in code. Here, take a look at it.'

Sam was nodding excitedly. He laid his hat on the floor, and studied the faces of the three men in turn. 'I'll be glad to work for you, judge. In fact, I consider it a privilege to be associated with you in anyway at all. Havin' seen the face of the killer will help.'

He took the sheet of paper which Vilman handed to him, and the room went silent as he studied it. At first he turned it this way and that, but juggling with it did no good. So he turned it back to the way it was handed to him and frowned at it afresh.

NXXGX XXRF SX YTRXFFXG
XXJ XLTTXL WVG.

He began: 'Grout's initials at the end. Otherwise, all consonants. No vowels. Too many Xs. Maybe the Xs ought to be vowels. They're *substitutes* for vowels! Give me a minute or two.'

Sherman chuckled in appreciation, in spite of the seriousness of the occasion. 'Hold on a minute, young fellow. You can take that with you to your hotel room. I'm sure you'll solve it in a short while. Meantime, we ought to give you some instructions. I'll tell you what I think. The others can add anything else.'

Sam looked up, nodded and smiled, his lips working soundlessly on the words of the puzzling code.

'I think you should start out cautiously by investigatin' the man who stole your horse. Almost certainly he killed Grout, but we can't be absolutely certain. No one has a greater respect for the law than I have. You have to be sure, Sam. He is probably headed for West Flats, a settlement due west of Bridgetown on the other side of a loop in the creek. That was where we had to send the ransom money and the information built up against the gangs.'

'If this man killed Grout, it could have been a personal matter or something to do with the VIP formerly in charge of the gangs. Should you decide there's a link-up with my enemy, play him along, don't aim to have him arrested right away. He could lead you to others. If he does, be patient. I shan't know any peace of mind in this life until I know for sure the identity of my secret enemy. I need to have him eliminated along with any of his minions still active, or at least put away somewhere.'

Sam stopped blinking at the paper as the judge paused. The trio of old friends were wondering how closely this young newcomer had been following the judge's advice. He surprised them.

'I'm with you so far, judge. At this stage, it occurs to me that I might have to pass myself off as a criminal, otherwise I would be distrusted by the sort of people I seek to mix with.'

'That seems very likely, Sam. How do you react to such a possibility?' Sherman asked.

Before he could answer, Vilman had a few words of advice. 'Don't make the mistake of takin' the matter too lightly, Sam. If you have to act like you're in cahoots with them, you could be up against determined peace officers, such as Pete, here. You'd be a kind of a spy, you see, and at times you'd have to act like an outlaw.'

Sam's thoughts raced. 'I see that, Mr Vilman. From my readings of old newspapers, I have the names of two or three known renegades. Maybe I could use one of them to force an introduction. An' there's another thing . . . '

'So what is this other thing?' Sherman prompted gently.

'Those counterfeit bills I brought back from Bridgetown. I wondered if I might take them with me. It's only a hunch, but I have this feelin' they might come in useful if I'm dealin' with villains. Of course, if you think otherwise, I'll understand.'

The judge stopped massaging his paunch and waved his hand in an airy fashion. 'Hand them back to him, Walter. I'm sure he won't use them unless he has to. And while you're at it, give him a worthwhile retainer. After all, we have no idea how long his investigation will take. I'd say two hundred, for a start.'

Sam tried to chip in with a modest refusal of the handsome retainer, but Sherman silenced him with a gesture. 'Say no more, young man. Now, why don't we all adjourn to the hotel dining room an' take an early lunch together? It may be quite a while before we get the chance again.'

Stevens and Vilman seemed pleased to note that their friend's morale had improved, but Sam surprised them once more by declining.

'It's jest possible there could be an informer in this town. If there is, I think I shouldn't be too closely associated with you gents. I'll ask to be excused while I go away an' work on the code. I could send it in to you at the hotel if an' when it's solved. Do you think it would be in order for me to have the use of Grout's buckskin?'

Vilman, who was holding the door, quickly agreed. He pushed the pouch of counterfeit money back into Sam's hands. 'Don't get the home-made stuff mixed up with your retainer, Sam. I'll make sure the livery releases the buckskin to you right after the meal. Mind how you go.'

There was another quick handshake all round before Sam preceded his associates into the street.

*   *   *

Back in his hotel room, Sam threw himself on the bed and started to pore over the code. With a pencil and paper, he wrote down the words, missing out the Xs. His enthusiasm waned for a while. The word beginning with YTR baffled him. He cudgelled his brain for five minutes without thinking of a single word to fit it. He got up and paced the room, frowning at his reflection in the mirror over the chest of drawers.

He felt sure that he had been right about the Xs being vowels, but not a single word occurred to him with the Xs out. He returned to the bed and tried to fit in the letter E, which someone had told him recurred most often.

At last it occurred to him that if the second word had been written backwards he could make the word FREE. After that, it was easy. He rewrote the whole sentence starting at the end and working to the beginning. And then he had it.

Little Joe Gafferty is free again.

Bursting with excitement, he wrote a short letter on the back of the form explaining how he had arrived at the solution. He followed this up by suggesting that if he had important news to transmit he would send it by telegraph using the same code.

He finished with a few words of greeting and folded up the paper. Next, he packed his few travel items and took them down to the foyer: making use of a large envelope, he addressed it to the judge. Leaving it on the counter, he rang the bell, waited for the receptionist and paid his bill.

The female clerk picked up the envelope just as he was stepping out of doors. Fifteen minutes later, he was heading out of town on the back of the buckskin, having paused long enough to buy in extra ammunition and a few essential trail groceries. He had one regret: that he had not had a further chance to look upon Melissa Sherman before riding away into danger on her father's behalf.

6

Walter V. Grout's low-barrelled buck-skin had a lot of stamina, which suited Sam's purpose. He kept it going forward at a brisk walk for upwards of two hours, although the sun was hot in the early part of the afternoon and there was no one to say he had to keep going through the hottest hours of the day.

All the time he was riding over un-broken ground, roughly in a west-north-westerly direction, Sam was mulling over the surprises of the previous day and the meeting with the judge and his friends that morning. His fortunes had certainly changed for the better in a remarkably short space of time.

He said to himself several times: 'Little Joe Gafferty is free again.' But that meant Gafferty must have been 'inside.' He must have been apprehended at a relatively late date during the troubles.

This surprised him, because Little Joe Gafferty had been one of three names listed in a newspaper article as being on the run from one or other of the notorious gangs. Another of the names stuck in his memory. 'Colt Brogan.' For the life of him he could not remember the third, but he thought it of no consequence, although a good memory never came amiss in detective work.

He put his mind back to town. All through the discussion of Judge Sherman's earlier troubles no mention has been made as to who had broken into the *Clarion* office and wrecked the machinery. He supposed he could hardly expect them, three citizens with good names, to hint at their complicity in the matter. And yet he did not doubt that they were implicated.

During the conference in the lawyer's office, several of the deputized riders from the hunting posse with the deputy sheriff had returned to town looking tired and frustrated. The man they sought had eluded them. Sam found himself wondering how long it would take for him to locate the killer, or if he, too, would fail to find him.

In the event that Grout's killer remained unapprehended, he would have to think again: try for a new lead in the town of West Flats.

The intelligent buckskin had its own way of protesting when it was tired and a long way from the last drink. Sam put up with its mildly wayward tantrums for a few minutes and then gave in. He dismounted, loosened and rocked his saddle and gave the horse a drink out of his hat.

The dust around his legs and the heat of the day made him feel like a late siesta. He wondered if he should take time out. While he was pondering the matter, the greyish-yellow horse trotted off for a few yards and began to make a modest meal of a few tufts of yellowing bunch grass.

Sam crawled into the scant shade of a few scrub bushes, put his hat over his face and drifted off into a light sleep. He was unconscious for an hour. The distant warning rattle of a snake's tail roused him sufficiently for him to get up and continue his journey.

Although his efforts in the saddle brought out the perspiration and he tasted dust through his bandanna, he kept going for three hours. In fact, it was the distant sight of Pecos Creek which finally convinced him that he had covered enough ground for one day.

Horse and man bathed. The lone redhead fished until he caught two small silvery items with which to enrich his diet. He cooked them and ate them with relish, lingering over his coffee for a full half hour before looking around for something to pass the time until dusk. He recollected having bought his extra ammunition. Some of that would have to provide his recreation.

In a thin tree stand, he blasted off a score of shells, firing from the hip and aiming at small tree branches most of the time. To finish off, he made a few quick draws and made snap shots at rocks. He took time out to give his .45 a good clean, and then went to work with the strange Henry over a greater distance, aiming at objects on the far side of the creek.

When he finally turned in, he was satisfied that his skill with guns had not gone back on him.

★   ★   ★

Noon, the following day. Heat, flies: the dusty main street of yet another western community youthful in origin. West Flats had about four streets going one way and a couple of intersections. It had little to commend it to anyone riding through. And yet it was a significant landmark in the troubled past of the judge, and in the present, if Grout's killer had indeed headed that way.

Sam stroked the grime off his face. He felt guilty that he had not thought out any special course of action. The heat and the protracted riding had for once not prompted any sort of preparation. He thought he ought to have asked what the town's amenities were before leaving Conchas. It would have helped to know how many hotels, boarding houses and such the town boasted before his arrival.

After all, if his quarry happened to be around, he did not specially want to blunder right in upon him unannounced, especially after the way in which they had first met. A sudden bout of pessimism made him ride all the length of the town down the main street. As the thoroughfare petered out he did a loop and allowed his mount to plod back again down a parallel street.

Passing a modest house with an upper storey, a woman who came out to shake crumbs off a cloth grinned at the sourness of his expression.

'If you're lookin' for a place to stay, young fellow, I have a room for you. Too bad you missed the midday meal, but I could fix you up with a snack.

Away an' put up your horse, why don't you? An' if you lose your way, ask for Molly Bligh's house. Can you remember that, now?'

She was a shapely woman of forty with green eyes, freckles, and a tip-tilted nose. Her accent was that of Ireland. Hearing her, Sam began to feel better.

'Who'd want to remember a name like Molly Bligh?' he replied. 'I'll remember the wicked twinkle in your eye, though, an' I guess you're a fair cook! Give me the name of a livery!'

'Tom Cobbold at the far end of the street! Leave the horse with him an' hurry back. I'll take coffee with you myself!'

The woman thought of shouting after him to ask what his name was, but she thought better of it in case her forwardness put him off. He was back in ten minutes, and sharing a green-painted bench with her in the narrow strip of back garden belonging to the house.

As Sam sipped the coffee, he said: 'I'm Sam Gould. Don't know how long I'll be stoppin'. It's a matter of business. One night, or maybe a few. It all depends if I find a friend.'

'All right, Sam, I'll buy that. Drink your coffee and take the weight off your mind. I'm a widow, used to the ways of men. Describe your friend, unless you want to tell me his name?'

Sam shook his head. Molly Bligh frowned a little, wrinkling her forehead under the golden curls which spilled down upon it from either side of a centre parting. Her left hand strayed to the square-cut neckline of her short-sleeved blue and white summer dress.

'Will you tell me one thing, Sam? You're not a bounty hunter, are you?'

'No, Molly, I'm not that. I can't tell you the fellow's name. Among other things, he borrowed my horse without askin' an' left me tied to a tree. But I can describe him to you.'

He concentrated for a moment, in order to give a full description. In his mind's eye, he saw again the stony look in the blue eyes, the thick long fair hair, the stubbled full face, the yellow bandanna and the buckskin outfit. He reeled them off.

Mrs Bligh's face was a picture of fleeting emotions until he came to the attire. And then she sighed luxuriously, grounded her empty coffee cup and stifled a yawn with her hand.

'Oh, Sam, me lad, for a few moments you had me goin'. My husband was a tall man with a lot of fair hair an' blue eyes. But he never did dress in any buckskin outfit, because he was a policeman in Chicago. He died tryin' to sort out a quarrel. Stopped the bullet meant for another man. I've yearned for another like my Paddy, but they're few an' far between. None of the men in the house right now are half as handsome as he was, savin' yourself!'

Sam stiffened and blushed at the sudden compliment. His landlady noticed the flush of colour and a melodious laugh rippled out of her which shook her bosom under the dress. At last, she got her breath back.

'Tell me, Sam, will you be after a wash an' a lie down on your bed, or do you have to go out an' look for your friend right away?'

'I'd like a wash, but I can't rightly settle down to rest until I've taken a look around.'

'All right, then. You can use the pump right away, if you've a mind to, an' your room is up there, over the kitchen. Call me if you want anything. I lay on the meal about six.'

Sam thanked her, waited for her to go indoors and then pulled off his shirt and moved under the pump. He dried himself off on the soiled shirt, slipped through the house and up to his room. A few minutes later, he moved out again. Two of the rooms were occupied. He could tell by the snores.

Bearded Tom Cobbold, the livery-man, had an understanding with the widow Bligh. She sent him customers and he did the same for her. Sam explained that he had taken a room at Molly's, and asked about a black stallion. No such horse had arrived in Tom's place, but he explained the locations of the other three livery stables in town. They were situated on the extremities of two central thoroughfares.

At the opposite end to the Cobbold establishment, he drew a blank and began to move around into the next street. There, again, he was unlucky. Traipsing around in the heat made him think. Obviously, all relevant information appertaining to the elusive killer would have been sent by telegraph to West Flats. The redhead began to wonder if there was anything in the town worth finding out about. Already he had asked questions in four places. No luck. No one knew about a black stallion or a man in a buckskin outfit. As he neared the fourth spot, Sam wondered if he wouldn't have to drop the horse and the killer questions and ask instead about a known name. That of Little Joe Gafferty. Maybe that would stir a few memories.

The door of the fourth stable stood open. The gaping hole was sufficient invitation for Sam to ease his way inside and take a look at the horses occupying the stalls on either side. He eyed them all briefly, looking for his stallion and at the same time weighing them up as to size and performance.

The head and shoulders of the man in charge appeared over the side wall of the last stall on the left.

'The name's Rick Yale. I'm in charge while the Boss is away. I don't believe you've got a horse in here, but a man can be interested in another man's animal an' still be honest. What can I do for you?'

Yale had short fair receding hair and eroded grey eyes pinched in at the corners. A strong nose and a lined face also helped to make him look older than his thirty-six years. His way of speaking suggested that he had been born in Scotland.

Sam moved clear of the stalls and would have shaken the other's hand, but he had a hay fork in the right and did not seem at all inclined to discard it.

'I was lookin' for a black stallion. About sixteen hands. A friend rode north on it a day or so ahead of me. Said he might dispose of it in West Flats. You'll not have seen such a horse?'

'There's no such beast here right now, mister, but the Boss did a business deal with a local rancher yesterday mornin' shortly before he left town. He took in a pinto. That's it, third on your right. The fellow wanted a bigger horse. Took the black away with him.'

'You don't know who it was, whether I could get in touch with him, do you?'

Yale frowned, giving his face a wolfish expression. He also scratched his scalp before answering. 'Ain't no reason for secrecy, I suppose. It was the representative of the Circle W who took the horse. Mr Weldon's ranch. You'll have heard the family name, I guess.

'The Boss used to figure in the

territorial legislature. Had a brother, powerful man in politics. Said to be close to the governor. The brother, that is. The local man didn't ever rate quite so high. So, if you want to see the stallion again, that's where it is. I'll have to ask you to leave, if that's all?'

Sam thanked him heartily and came out. It began to look as if the killer had done a trade with the real owner of the livery before this man, Yale, took over. Now, he had something to go on. *If* he was onto the right horse. The Circle W could be visited. Someone might know something about the man who brought the black to town.

And he could also make enquiries about Little Joe Gafferty. A sudden spurt of interest kept him on the move around the buildings which were open in spite of the heat of early afternoon.

The name of Little Joe Gafferty did not mean much to anyone. Some thought it had a familiar ring, but could not recall where they had heard it.

Others shook their heads, declining to search their memories in the heat. It was not until he met up with old Tom Cobbold again in a saloon that he made any real headway. Tom gulped down a third of a pint of beer after hearing the question.

'Gafferty? Let me see. Yes, there was a Sam Gafferty in this town a few years back. Kept a business of some sort. Had two boys. Little Joe, you say? He'd be the younger one. Very tall an' powerfully built. Like a young bear. Old Sam died, of course. His widow went back east somewhere. And his boys left the town, went on their travels, I guess you'd say. Ain't seen or heard anything of them since.'

Sam talked around the subject for a minute or two, but soon perceived that there was nothing more to be learned from the liveryman.

One or two other enquiries failed to raise any further information, and Sam gradually lost interest in his questioning. He retired to Molly Bligh's house at an early hour, enjoyed a good meal and permitted himself to be entertained at a later hour when his landlady sang to a piano played by a travelling salesman who also had a room with her.

When he retired for the night, all his thoughts were on a trip to the Circle W ranch, and the possible recovery of his stolen horse.

7

It was nearly ten o'clock the next morning when Sam walked the borrowed buckskin over the hoof-pocked ground on the east side of the cluster of buildings which formed the headquarters of the Circle W spread. Already the animal had grown used to him. It had a habit of flicking its dark tail sideways and doing a sidestep when it was in a good mood, and its spirits certainly seemed to be high on this occasion.

In the distance, there were the usual signs of activity. A man moving between the long low bunkhouse and the cookhouse next door. Another cleaning out a stable, and the sound of a hammer striking metal in the smithy. A Mexican woman was in the act of cleaning the windows of the house on a short ladder.

All these goings on were noted by the

newcomer, but already most of his attention was centred upon a young couple exercising a horse in the corral on the near side of the buildings. His pulse quickened on two counts. He had recognized at once the missing black, and the girl who was squatting decoratively on the top rail of the corral had a shape to draw the eyes of any man.

Instead of heading straight for the house and making his wants known, he slowed the buckskin and headed boldly for the horse arena. The girl glanced at him and then promptly looked away, while her male companion showed the black a fence of perhaps five feet in height and attempted to make it jump.

The rider was long, lean and fair: perhaps a couple of years older than Sam. His long legs were tightly clamped round the barrel of the black and his cleanshaven face was a tight mask of frustration as the animal refused and backed off. Sam halted his mount a few feet away from the rail and slowly dismounted. All the time he was busy his eyes were on the young couple.

The girl's luxurious crop of golden blonde hair spilled out around her shoulders from under a cream-coloured flat-crowned stetson perched squarely on her head. She had on a tailored pale blue shirt with twin lace-fringed pockets. A pair of darker blue jeans hugged her hips and accentuated the length of her legs, which ended in half boots. She had a pretty, spoiled expression. Her full lips suggested that she pouted rather easily.

The girl said: 'Try him again, Joe. He ain't used to you yet!'

Joe turned the black in a tight circle, nodded grimly to the girl and glared momentarily at Sam without saying anything. He had on a dun stetson with the brim rolled to a point above his bony forehead. His smart brown shirt and yellow bandanna set off his physique and gave the impression that he belonged to the owning family, rather than being a hired hand.

A touch of the rowels sent the black forward again, but once more it refused at the last moment and veered off to one side.

Sam walked across to the rail and rested his elbows on the middle row of horizontal poles. He touched his hat to the girl, and nodded towards the horse and rider.

'Good day to you, miss. My name is Sam Gould. I'm wonderin' if your friend would let me have a ride on the black. You see, I've met the animal before, an' I'm sure I could make him do the jumps. Something's buggin' him at the moment.'

The girl turned reluctantly to face Sam, shooting a searching glance at him, her grey eyes shaded by her hat brim. She shrugged rather prettily, and turned to face the rider who had heard what Sam had said on account of the latter having raised his voice for that purpose.

Joe glanced sideways at Sam, his sullen expression hostile. He started to say: 'I don't see how — '

But the girl interrupted him. 'Aw, go on, Joe. It can't do any harm. Let the stranger have a go. After all, some horses are mighty tricky in new surroundings.'

Joe sniffed. Sam favoured him with a fetching smile. The girl crossed her booted legs in another provocative position. Abruptly, the rider slipped his left foot out of the stirrup. He swung his right leg up and over the saddle pommel and dropped to the ground.

'All right, then, stranger, give it a go.'

'I'm obliged to you, mister,' Sam returned eagerly.

The redhead ducked through the poles, walked up to the black and tucked his shoulder under its head. It had recognized him at once. For a few seconds it rubbed its muzzle against him and snickered with pleasure.

Sam murmured: 'It's been a long time, boy.'

Already he was wondering if he would take the black with him when he left the spread. He had been fond of it for a long time, and the parting had been an emotional wrench.

'Let's see if you've forgotten your tricks.'

He mounted it from the right side, an act familiar to the horse. The saddle under him was not his own. Since he and the black were parted the saddle and other horse trappings had been changed. Even in the unfamiliar leather, it felt good to be mounted on the stallion again. He walked it off round the corral, feeling it respond under him. It trotted at the slight hint he gave it. He halted it on the far side, directly opposite the young couple, and gave it a long look at the jumping barrier.

'We're goin' up an' over, boy, so take your time an' make it look good.'

The black rolled its neck and tossed its head. Then it was walking forward. Some ten yards short of the fence it broke into a trot. Sam assessed its progress. Although he was anxious, he did not think that it had suffered any sort of strain. It ought to jump the five-foot peeled pole with ease.

'All right, let's go!'

Sam adjusted his position in the saddle, the black took off and surged upwards. One of its rear shoes lightly scraped the pole without dislodging it, and then they were down again and easing up in the direction of the watching couple.

The girl clapped two or three times and then stopped abruptly. Her male escort said nothing and showed no special interest. Sam made a tight turn and did the return run to the obstacle at a slightly quicker speed. Again, the black jumped well and landed easily, stirring up a slight flurry of dust.

Sam could guess at the reactions of the young man who had not coped very well, but now he did not want to have to give up the black at once. At the other side, he called: 'If you care to raise the bar another six inches, I think we could make it! Suit yourself, though!'

The young couple were whispering quietly together. At the same time, an older man started to approach the corral from the direction of the ranch house. The newcomer was slightly above average height with a bulky rounded figure. His skin was that of a sixty-year old who had spent much of his time out of doors. A short neat grey beard adorned his chin while the lack of any hair along the temples and around the back of his head revealed that his skull, under the black stetson, was shaved. His neat black frockcoat and matching trousers made his legs seem short and partially hid his bulk.

He walked without haste, his black eyes taking in every detail of the scene, a cigar bobbing slightly between his full lips. He was heading for the observers. Just before he reached them, the girl jumped down off the rail and trotted with a characteristic outward swing of her forearms towards the obstacle.

She stretched up at one end of the pole and raised it the suggested amount with the eyes of the three men watching her every movement. When she had raised the other end, she backed off a couple of paces, waved to Sam and stood with her hands planted lightly on her hips.

Sam was as aware as she was herself of the animal grace in her movements. He hoped she would not distract him sufficiently to make him spoil the jump.

He murmured: 'Three spectators now, boy. At least one of them wants to see us fail. Take a good look at that bar. Tread carefully.'

He only became aware of his words at the end of his utterance, and what he had said surprised him. With an effort, he shrugged off the tension which was building up in him. It was not a matter of life and death whether he cleared the obstacle. His apprehension surprised him. He supposed it was the presence and interest of the pretty girl which was affecting him. He shrugged his shoulders and slackened the muscles of his legs. Twice he nudged the black's flanks with his boots and then they were off.

This time the horse accelerated earlier. It lengthened its stride, positioned itself with care and leapt. Sam hung on, his back arched and his youthful freckled expression hidden under a mask of concentration. The bar sailed past beneath them, and then they were down with the black going away and gradually slowing.

A pair of horny hands clapped in appreciation of his performance. As he circled the arena, the girl ran to her kinsfolk and scrambled back upon the rails. Breathing hard, the redhead walked his mount towards them, a nervous smile on his face.

The older man stepped through the rails and advanced to meet him as he dismounted. Their hands came together in a firm handshake.

'That was a fine piece of ridin', young fellow. Best I've seen in a long time. By the way, I'm Hank Weldon. I own this ranch, although others run it for me these days. Meet my nephew and niece, Joe and Anne Riddall.'

'I'm Sam Gould, formerly of Amarillo, in the state of Texas. I came to see you, Mr Weldon, on account of some information I picked up in West Flats. Maybe we could go some place an' talk for a few minutes.'

Weldon's intense black eyes were ranging over him all the time, taking in details of his weight, his muscles and the way he carried himself. Sam flapped his fawn vest, aware that his green shirt was soiled with perspiration and dust, and yet his host seemed to be favouring him with grudging admiration.

'Come on into the house, Sam. You as well, Joe an' Anne. Joe, have one of the hands see to that buckskin an' put the black in the stable for us. He's had enough exercise for one day.'

Weldon gripped Sam tightly by the arm and led him off towards the big hacienda. Anne followed them a little distance behind, while her brother, Joe, diverged long enough to call a man from the bunkhouse.

Presently, they were all sitting in a roomy dining-room, liberally filled with comfortable furniture. There was expensive covering on the floor and colourful curtains at the windows. Weldon received a tray of cups and saucers from a Mexican serving woman, while Joe Riddall produced a bottle of whisky and glasses from a glass-fronted cabinet. He poured for the three men, leaving out his sister, who sat by a window sipping coffee. Hatless, she looked more attractive than ever and her frank open grey eyes were scarcely ever off Sam's face.

A few minutes passed, during which the men drank and smoked. Eventually, the owner's burning curiosity prompted him to ask the visitor's business.

'After your hospitality, Mr Weldon, I find it hard to tell why I came. The truth is I was set upon by a stranger between towns. This jasper made off with my horse, leavin' me tied to a tree. The horse in question was the black I've been ridin' out there. A liveryman in town remembered his master havin' sold someone from this ranch a black stallion such as I described to him. And that's why I'm here.'

A stony silence engulfed the room, so that the sounds of two women laundering clothes in the rear part of the building was clearly audible. Anne gasped, and looked hurt. Joe's face was a mask of incredulity, while the expression on Weldon's face changed with great subtlety. The owner's innermost thoughts would have been of more than passing interest to a thought reader. His black eyes, scarcely ever still under the jutting brows, gave a hint of the powerful emotions the man was capable of.

In a flash of comprehension, Sam realized that it was Weldon and not the girl who had created the tension in him out there in the corral. Now, he had the feeling that Weldon was very displeased, although the poker face did not show it.

'That explains why Gould could make the stallion jump so successfully when I couldn't,' Joe murmured. There

111

was a kind of relief in his voice.

Anne was looking out of the window as words of protest escaped her mobile lips. 'All the same, that horse was bought in good faith an' that has to mean something.'

Weldon chuckled drily. 'So you came all the way to the Weldon ranch in the hope of receivin' back a stolen horse, did you? I won't insult you by sayin' I don't believe it was ever yours. Your story is an unusual one, but strange things happen between towns, even in this county. My niece, there, unfortunately, has taken a great likin' to the horse. You must excuse her bad manners.'

Anne turned to glare at her uncle, but, like many others, she found Weldon's concentrated stare too much for her. After a few seconds, she blushed and looked away. 'It's your horse, uncle, an' you are the one who will say what happens to it.'

So saying, she stood up, pouted and stalked out of the room. As soon as she had gone from view, Weldon chuckled.

'What do you say, Joe?' the uncle asked. 'Even if we insisted in keepin' the black, it might not take to you. Even before Sam, here, arrived we had learned it had a will of its own. Would it be fair to keep it?'

At this stage, Sam offered his opinion. Why he spoke as he did, he was not quite sure. He had real affection for the black. 'I'd say it would be fair to keep the black, although it's been my constant companion for a long time. I suppose you don't know any details of the man who lodged it in the livery?'

Weldon shook his head very decidedly. 'No, Sam, I can't help you in that direction, but if you're prepared to leave the black with us for the sake of Anne, I'd like to reimburse you. I'm not a poor man. I have other horses. You could choose one. We'll have another whisky an' then go take a look at the ridin' horses in the far corral.'

At this suggestion, Sam's embarrassment slipped from him. He found himself talking easily with Joe, who had been stiff and withdrawn up to this time. Presently, they strolled out of doors again, and Weldon proudly showed three more riding horses, all of which would have fetched as much as the black in an auction.

In the corral on the west side of the buildings were a big grey, its colourful hide peppered with black markings: a young chestnut with a lot of running and riding to do was making spirited runs around the limits of the corral: watching the other two from a distance was a beautiful white mare which looked to have a lot of superb breeding in its ancestry.

For a time, the three men stood close to the rail and merely feasted their eyes on the quadrupeds. Sam's eyes were on the other two men, as well as the animals. He had noticed a sharp eye glance pass between Weldon and his nephew. Nothing was to be said as to which member of the family favoured each horse.

'Well, Sam, I don't suppose you've ever had an offer quite like this before. Make your choice. Feel free to speak your mind. You've made a sacrifice an' I'm prepared to do the same. What do you say?'

Sam grinned and murmured his appreciation of what was being done for him. He knew he would be thought a fool if he didn't choose. And yet if his choice angered this formidable rancher, he had a feeling that a lot of trouble could come of it.

He guessed that the big grey was Weldon's horse. The mare, he saw as a woman's choice: probably bought specially for the girl, Anne. The chestnut he associated with Joe. It needed a firm rider. Maybe Joe would be better suited with the black when he had mastered it.

'If you're sure you want to go through with this deal, Mr Weldon I'll take the chestnut,' Sam decided, his voice showing conviction.

He was relieved when he found that his choice had pleased both his

115

companions. They banged him on the back and hurried him indoors for more whisky. He was forced to stay to lunch, which was a good meal of three courses. The talk was easy, and even Anne managed to be gracious to him as he told in a gauche fashion tales of his minor adventures between towns.

By the time Sam elected to leave, the food and drink and the broiling heat of the sun had taken a lot of energy out of the four of them. They parted where they had first come together, by the rail of the corral on the east side of the spread.

Sam shook hands with Weldon and Joe Riddall and exchanged a personal parting word with Anne, who was holding the halter of the chestnut. Feeling suddenly embarrassed, he quickly mounted up on the buckskin and touched his hat.

'Don't go takin' any wooden coins,' Weldon ribbed him. 'If I ever hear who stole the black from you, I'll try to let you know.'

Sam thanked him, knowing the

promise was an empty one because Weldon had no idea of his future movements. They watched him out of sight, waving as he disappeared into trees. Joe and Anne, reading their uncle's mood, left him where he was and hurried into the house.

Presently, Weldon strolled over to the stable where the black was and stared at it. He blinked rapidly several times, mildly troubled in his thoughts. He was annoyed. Mostly, he was thinking that it had been a fool thing to do to have *that* particular horse brought out to the ranch.

8

The redhead's thoughts were in something of a turmoil during most of the time it took to get back into the town of West Flats. He kept seeing again the formidable owner of the lush spread and his two young relations. Weldon was unusual in Sam's experience. He emitted an aura of some sort which proved at the same time to be intriguing and off-putting.

Although the rancher seemed to be about sixty, and was by his own admission more or less retired, yet Sam felt that he had a tremendous store of nervous energy and that his feelings ran deep. Furthermore, the young Texan had the impression that the young couple were wary of him, kin or no kin.

If Weldon was as strong a character as he assumed, then the interview about the horse could very well have taken a much more difficult turn. Sam found himself wondering why he had not asked questions about Little Joe Gafferty, and why he had not said anything about his associations in Conchas — his involvement with the newspaper and his work as an investigator. Although he had told stories about his travels, he had kept back from his hosts the real reason for his moving out.

About the time when he thought of taking the saddle off the back of the buckskin and trying it for a change on the back of the chestnut, he began to think forward. Already, in his mind, he was writing off as a lead the man in the buckskin outfit who had attacked him.

Therefore, any further leads in the area might have to depend upon shaking down further information about former outlaws. It might have been something to do with the change of motion on the back of the promising chestnut which gave him his new idea. He wondered why he had not thought of it before, especially with his own private interests to hint at it. He would advertise. There was a local paper in West Flats, although its circulation was not very large.

A small ad, purporting to come from a known name in the old ring of outlaws might just do the trick. He found himself smiling as his mind warmed to the idea. Moreover, the weekly edition of the paper, the *West Flats Mercury*, was due out on the street the following day, or at the very latest the day after. That meant he had to get his notice in the paper as soon as he arrived.

Two things occupied his mind as he completed the rest of the journey into town. The actual words of the personal message, and the names he had read among the old copies of the Conchas City *Clarion:* names referring to outlaws of yesteryear, or earlier.

★   ★   ★

The return to town presented no problems. Cobbold looked after the two horses. Molly Bligh took him back into her home and made him welcome. She had a look in her eye which suggested that she would have liked him for her favourite lodger, but she did not press him for details of his future movements. She guessed he had old scores to settle.

A poker-faced ageing male jack-of-all-trades at the *Mercury* took his small contribution for the personal column, and Sam found it printed substantially as he had submitted it high in the column on the third of four pages.

He was out and about the day after his return, anxious to grab a copy at the earliest opportunity. So speedily did he move down the intersection when he heard the newsboy's cry that the barefooted youngster cannoned straight into him and lost most of his papers on the ground.

The lad seemed upset, until Sam insisted upon taking the only soiled one himself, and actually assisted in recovering the others.

Sam stepped into the shade of a sidewalk awning, the time being three o'clock in the afternoon. There, he read again the words of his own composition.

An old friend of Little Joe Gafferty, formerly associated with the town of West Flats, would dearly like to be put in touch.

'Signed': Colt Brogan.

For the first time in his life he had used the name of another: that of a known outlaw. Colt Brogan, according to the record, had fled to South America when local law enforcement bodies had cracked down upon the gangs. Sam had no idea what he looked like, and he hoped this shot into the unknown would not end in disaster. There were so many imponderables. For instance, Little Joe Gafferty and Colt Brogan might have been sworn enemies. He shuddered, and felt quite despondent as he strolled back to the boarding house, needing to hear the cheering Irish voice of Molly Bligh.

He was chopping firewood for Molly's stove around ten in the morning when the idea came to him that he would not be able to wait a whole week for a possible reply to his notice. The blade of the axe passed very close to his thumb as his thoughts wandered. There was a chance that he would not have to. He smiled to himself as he reflected that the overriding excitement had dimmed his judgement. In order to reply to 'Colt Brogan' the receiver of the message would have to contact the newspaper office. Even if the unknown person only offered a verbal message. Maybe the reply would come in less than a week!

His stomach crawled with excitement at the possibilities which a definite reply would put before him. He strolled back indoors with the firewood and stacked it around the foot of the kitchen stove, not noticing that Molly was framed in the doorway which led to the rest of the house.

Suddenly he became aware of her. He turned quickly and surprised a look of longing on her pleasing features. The black apron which protected her dress had ridden up on her hips, where her hands were planted.

'My word, Sam, me lad, you're a deep one an' all. You were miles away in your thoughts when you came in. I can't help wonderin' sometimes what it is that motivates you.'

He straightened up and shrugged. 'If fate is kind to me, Molly, maybe one day I'll tell you. Right now, I can't. I have a job of work to do an' it could take a long time.'

★ ★ ★

In the newspaper office, the clerk studied him with renewed interest when he went along that afternoon.

'Colt Brogan, you say, young fellow? Well, as it happens, we found an envelope pushed through the door when we opened up this morning. Here it is. No extra charge.'

Sam thanked him and came away, fingering the envelope as though its contents were priceless. In the privacy of his own room, he opened it up and marvelled at its contents. He had in his possession a small sketch map, neatly drawn in pencil and showing the location of a remote cabin some five miles north-east of West Flats, on the other side of Pecos Creek, which could be crossed by a ford.

That night he ate heartily, and sang to the piano. It came as no surprise to Mollie when he told her before turning in that he was riding out of town after breakfast, and that he did not know when he would be back.

Before he gave himself over to the serious matter of sleep, he composed a short message intimating that he expected to make contact with his missing friend north of West Flats. He decided to address it to Vilman and to leave it unsigned. Five minutes was all the time necessary to translate it into the code known to his contacts in Conchas City. He would take the message to the telegraph office just prior to leaving town.

★ ★ ★

The log cabin was in a glade, hidden on two sides by mixed stands of oak and pine trees. Not far away on the north side was a useful grassed hollow where horses could be hidden. At eleven in the morning, it all looked quiet and peaceful, but Sam's senses were keenly on the alert. He was forking the chestnut, having decided to leave the buckskin behind for the time being, in case he encountered anyone who knew its owner.

No one appeared as he rode up to the shack, although he whistled and did his best to attract the attention of anyone who was near. The blood was pounding through his veins as he dismounted, looped the reins round the chestnut's neck and walked purposefully towards the door on the near side. The windows were clean, but no human faces appeared to examine the newcomer.

He knocked on the door, received no answer and finally turned the handle and pushed it open. His nostrils told him that food had been eaten that morning, but the dishes and cups had been washed and stacked in wall side racks. His troubled eyes took in the two two-tier bunks, the stove and its pipe, a table and chairs. Out of his eye corner, he saw the end of an open loft.

A couple of hats hung from long nails knocked into a wall. There were three rifles similarly hanging. He moved further inside, began a slow walk, thinking that he needed to survey the outside again through the windows.

Without warning, his neck hairs began to prickle. He felt for certain that a man's eyes were upon him. In one sudden movement, he pulled the .45 Colt which hung habitually at his right side, and sprang about looking for another human. His gun made two small arcs before he lined it up on the upper part of a man's head just showing above the loft end.

Thick tousled fair hair, a wrinkled forehead. Two stony blue eyes ranged behind a long-barrelled revolver pointing straight at his head. Perspiration sprang from his forehead. He cleared his dry throat as his intelligence told him he had seen this man before.

'What sort of a welcome is this when a man has been invited to call?'

The menacing gun above him stayed right where it was, but the man behind it shifted his head and shoulders ever so slightly, so that more of his face showed and the bulking fringes on his shoulders. The man who had previously stolen his horse now laughed, confirming his identity.

He ground out: 'Colt Brogan was welcome, but that ain't your name, amigo, so I've no reason to back off!'

Working hard to keep his own gun

steady, Sam retorted: 'I came to see Little Joe Gafferty, an' that makes us even. At least, *I* can explain how an' why I'm here. *You're* not Little Joe! I'd lay a wager on it!'

A deep fruity voice, scarcely more than a whisper, cut through the critical tension between the two men. It came from the door by which Sam had entered. 'Oh, I don't know, Jake. It's always nice to hear what a fellow has to say. After all, we can fix him up with a dose of lead poisonin' any time we feel like it.'

The man who had surprised both of them was tall and heavily built. The crown of his hat scarcely cleared the top of the door, but there was no time at the outset to weigh him up more closely. The briefest glance showed that he was pointing a pair of twin .44s at Sam, one held at either side of the spreading waistline flanking the barrel chest in its khaki-coloured shirt.

Sam, who was still leaking perspiration, read the situation thoroughly. He was the first to lower his weapon. He moved very slowly with his arms outstretched, until he was able to put it down quietly on top of the table. The head and shoulders of Jake appeared and his gun was withdrawn.

Sam said: 'You must be Little Joe Gafferty, the man I came to see. I don't know if you planned all this, but I'm glad you stepped in jest when you did.'

So as not to further the tension in the room, Sam moved around the table and seated himself out of reach of his discarded gun. The man in the doorway kept his stance for a while longer and then stepped indoors and holstered his weapons with one of the smoothest actions Sam had ever seen.

'I'm Little Joe, an' this here is Jake Mayo, an associate of mine. You won't mind if I hang your gun away out of harm's reach till we get to know one another a little better, will you now?'

Sam's revolver was removed and hung on a wall nail by its trigger guard. Jake Mayo lowered the ladder into place and came down it, his rugged face partially transformed by a twisted grin. Little Joe moved around, this way and that. Eventually, he came to rest on the lower level of one of the two sets of bunks.

'How come you used Colt Brogan's name, and what do you want with me?'

'I met Colt Brogan on my travels. In a small country in South America. We were workin' at a hacienda. The other cowpunchers used a bolas. Neither Colt nor I were much good with the bolas at first. But we worked at it until we were as capable as the rest.

'Bein' a couple of outsiders, we were thrown together. We talked at times. He said if I ever came to this part of the states to look you up. You would offer me a job. That's about all. I'm back, an' here I am.'

All this time, Sam was drawing on what he could remember of the sketchy background notes outlined in a newspaper article about Brogan and others. He knew that from this time forward he would have to be very careful in what he said. His life would probably depend upon it.

Mayo stretched out his long legs on the bench opposite Sam and puckered his brow as he thought of possible questions.

Mayo said: 'What did Brogan look like, an' where is he now?'

'I don't know where he is now. He suddenly got restless an' took off for other parts. As for his appearance, I don't know how he looked when he was with you. When I knew him, he had a lot of hair on his face. He looked to me like a man tryin' to change his appearance. Maybe *you* can tell *me* where he is now. I'd like to meet up with him again.'

Sam glanced from one to the other. If Brogan had returned and was in touch with this lethal pair, he knew they would discover that he was lying. Neither of the other two ventured an answer. Judging by their expressions, they did not know anything more about Brogan's recent movements. He had the impression that if he talked, it might put them off asking more questions. He turned his attention to Mayo.

'You left me in a difficult position between towns, Jake, when you took my horse. I suppose you don't have it with you any more?'

Mayo glanced sideways at Little Joe. Presently, he started to laugh. 'Nope, I don't have that big black any more. But it did come in handy for a while. Maybe I'll be in a position to do you a favour, one of these days.'

Little Joe remained passive, weighing up this new revelation and figuring how it affected the present situation.

Sam said: 'You could help by offerin' me some food. It's a long time since breakfast. How about it?'

Mayo shrugged and yawned. After a while, Little Joe gave his approval. Mayo put on the coffee pot and boosted the fire in the stove. Sam felt that the first crisis was over. They were accepting him, but he was on a sort of probation. The testing time lay in the future.

They would be bound to put him to some sort of a test before they could be sure he was trustworthy. Sam's nerve-wracking spy role had begun.

9

The rest of that day dragged for Sam. He found Little Joe a moody character to deal with, and it was only when he remembered the text of the coded telegraph message that he had the clue to the big man's present attitude to life. Gafferty had been in prison. He had grown used to long periods of silence, and to his own company.

Even Mayo showed signs of irritation when Gafferty failed to communicate in the normal way, and he was glad to agree when Sam suggested a few hands of cards. While they played at the table, Joe wiled away the evening reclining on his bunk and smoking cigarette after cigarette.

As Sam played, he marvelled that he was sharing the company of his own attacker, a man who had almost certainly murdered the former Pinkerton operative and who therefore had been responsible for getting him the undercover job he was on. There had to be others involved in this conspiracy against the judge. Someone must have tipped off Mayo that Grout was on his way to make contact with the old enemy.

And Grout, if he had sent the coded telegraph message, clearly thought that Gafferty was a force to be reckoned with again.

Sam wondered what they were waiting for. Was it for the arrival of their leader, or were they short of an idea for putting him to the test? The other two shared one two-tier bunk that night, while Sam had a lower bunk to himself.

The young redhead only slept fitfully, but nothing happened to disturb the peace of the night hours, and no one was moving when Sam finally awoke to the new day and its dangers. Mayo was still sleeping, but Gafferty, his body still geared to prison routine, had been awake for some time although he made no effort to get up.

Sam did some elaborate yawning. Before Mayo was properly roused, Sam had his boots on and was checking the stove. He raked it well, making some noise and helping Mayo's return to full consciousness.

'I'll go an' get some firewood,' Sam remarked.

He went out, savoured the fresh air of a new day and took his time with the chore, figuring that if he gave the other two a chance to talk when he was not there, some sort of development might occur. They breakfasted off bacon and beans, and by the time the plates were empty, Mayo was prompting Gafferty to a staccato conversation.

'We've been thinkin' of payin' a short visit to Indian Wells for some time,' the fair man began. 'How would it be, Joe, if we made that visit today an' took Sam with us? Maybe he could make himself useful. What do you think?'

Gafferty burped, massaged his ample middle and agreed without enthusiasm. 'Sure. Seein' as how you intended to join us, Gould, you must have an idea what sort of business we're in. Tell me, did you go to South America because you like travellin' or did you *have* to go there?'

Sam perked up and smiled. 'I had to clear out. Made an unsuccessful attack on a coach. Got a lot of trouble on my backtrail. It happened because I was ridin' a horse that was easily spooked. I reckon Indian Wells is over on the east side of the creek, north of Bridgetown. Is that right?'

'That's right,' Mayo confirmed. 'Let's say we could do with some funds. We know a couple of good callin' places. You could show us how good you are at extractin' money without bringin' the law down on our necks. You *agreeable* to that?'

Sam kept the right sort of expression on his face, although he felt far from pleased at the latest suggestion. 'All right, if that's the way you want it. In this line of business, a man doesn't bring testimonials. He has to prove himself, I guess.'

Gafferty, to Sam's surprise, took a hand washing the pots and generally tidying up. While Mayo was out to collect the horses, he ventured a question. 'If I'm to take risks, I suppose you'll allow me to take my side-iron along with me?'

Gafferty stared at the revolver hanging on the wall. 'I guess so. Get it down an' wear it, only don't ever get the idea of usin' it to make bounty money out of us, 'cause no one ain't ever likely to turn Jake an' me in again. Understand?'

Sam nodded and collected his gun.

★ ★ ★

Indian Wells, which they reached before noon, proved to be a rather sleepy backwater of a town. Three streets, two intersections, total population between three and four hundred. Two saloons, a scattering of small shops, three liveries, a hotel and so on.

It took little more than ten minutes

to ride around the rutted streets and get a general view of the amenities. Sam found his nerves jumping, as he was completely in the dark as to what they expected him to do. He was pleased when they reined in before an adobe *cantina* in North Street and settled down to drink a few glasses of tepid beer.

All the other drinkers were Mexicans, who tended to keep to themselves aloof from white Americans at the other end of the room. This situation meant that the trio could easily talk unheard. Gafferty reduced his fruity voice to a whisper.

'North of here, standin' in their own ground, are a few houses belongin' to wealthy folks. There's one we know about called Casablanca, on account of the exterior is painted white. It belongs to a wealthy retired railroad official who is out of town.

'Although it's rumoured he goes off to the west coast to live it up fairly often, the whisper has it he leaves large sums of money hidden in his house. Jake an' me, we want you to get into the house, find the hidden hoard, bring it out an' rejoin us some little distance north of the west trail out of town. You want to ask any questions?'

'Is the house empty now?'

Mayo nodded, his stony eyes probing Sam's expression in search of his true feelings. Sam asked when it should be done.

'Not now,' Gafferty resumed. 'Not durin' siesta. It might be too obvious. Wait till four o'clock. You'll leave us when we quit this *cantina*. Make your own way there, when the time comes. Effect your own entry. We'll be around, probably somewhere along the front of the buildin' jest in case you're likely to be disturbed. That all right with you?'

Genuine doubts flitted across Sam's features as he weighed up the possibility of pulling off this unwanted task without getting himself into serious trouble. The other two waited. At length, he shrugged, rose to his feet, nodded and strolled out into the open air, where the oppressive heat of the sun greeted him.

He found a café on South Street, with a shaded strip round the back where the chestnut horse could wait and slake its thirst at a stone trough. While he was eating a substantial meal of beef, vegetables and fruit pie, Sam mulled over the situation. Did they really trust him or were they planning for something to happen to him during the raid on the empty house?

He couldn't tell, and no amount of conjecture would make him feel easier about it. He ate stolidly, wondering at his own appetite in the circumstances. Several possible schemes for having him apprehended occurred to him without much mental effort. He could only think of one really good reason why they would want the theft to succeed.

Money. All criminals were interested in cash. If there was a chance of reaping a rich reward, almost certainly they would back his efforts.

When he had drunk and eaten his fill, he paid the bill and wandered out at the back. There, he briefly groomed the chestnut and removed the saddle for a while to give it some relief. He yawned. Two hours of time to kill, and no better way in which to do it than sleeping. *If* his troubled conscience would allow it.

To his surprise, he did sleep, in spite of the unyielding surface of the bench which supported him.

★ ★ ★

Four o'clock came all too quickly. Sam roused himself with an effort, turned his mind back to Conchas City and the men who believed in him and what he was doing. He visualized the profiles of Judge Dan Sherman, Walter Vilman and Pete Stevens. They all seemed friendly enough, but exceedingly distant — as though seen through the wrong end of a spyglass.

He wondered what sort of advice they would have given him at a time like this when he was about to make an illegal entry, and probably commit his first robbery. He was doing it with the intention of winning the confidence of Gafferty and Mayo, but would a retired judge have expected him to take such a chance as this?

Sam shrugged. He tried to be cheerful about it. If he was careful, he might still manage to keep out of trouble. After all, most house-breakers and burglars were of fairly low intelligence. As this was likely to be his last break-in, he ought to make it a good one.

While his head cleared, he checked over all details of the chestnut's harness, still wondering how his chancy strike against the empty house would go. There were people walking about now. Somewhere a piano was being played. Further off a mongrel dog plagued by flies was moving around emitting plaintive yelps. In the main thoroughfare, a four-wheeled vehicle churned up the dirt of the street: a wheel creaked putting a rhythm to the dull thump of horseshoes and the jingle of harness. A man with strong lungs was whistling the tune 'Dixie' slightly off-key.

Sam formed his lips to match those of the distant whistler, but he remained silent. Savouring the last of the shade, he mounted up, turned the chestnut into the alley and emerged into the street. The heat hit him again and the time started to drag.

He moved across South Street, painfully conscious of himself and his horse, although there were very few people about, especially off the town centre. He kept his head down, trying to look unobtrusive and to give the appearance of having nowhere in particular to go.

No one paid any particular attention to him. Through the intersection and into Main. A guilty glance to his left to where the sign hung outside the peace office on the north side. A few more people moving about without speed, two or three horse-drawn conveyances. No sign of a man wearing a star, or of Mayo and Gafferty. He wondered how they had passed the rest of the afternoon.

Across North Street with the slanting rays of the sun probing for him between one set of buildings and the other. The chestnut speeded up a little. Perhaps a bit of Sam's restlessness had communicated itself to the beast.

Shadow again, and a left turn. Further north, beyond his line of ride, one of the exclusive residences, tree-lined and expensive-looking. He rode on, aware of an empty avenue of cottonwoods going by on his right, but already his attention was ahead of the trees and focused on the building known as Casablanca.

No signs of his partners. A man and a woman in a surrey came down from the north beyond Casablanca, heading across the intersections for the other side of town. For upwards of a minute, Sam studied the white house, looking for the least signs of movement. He saw none, other than the gentle movement of foliage.

He turned in the saddle, pretending to grope in his saddle bag. All was still behind him, at the east end of town. On then, with a solid wooden block on his left containing a saloon, a boarding house and two or three offices. No sounds on that side, largely because he was seeing the backs of the buildings. On the other side, a white wooden rail fence along the front of Casablanca to a height of three feet.

The plot was long and rectangular with its long sides facing east and west. Almost a third of it, the ground nearest the avenue of cottonwoods, was given over to an ornamental garden with miniature trees, two ponds and a small pagoda-like building.

The upper part of the two-storey building, which had dormer attics facing east and west, towered above a high hedge on the west side of the garden. In front was a narrow lawn, fronting a verandah almost completely filled by a swinging seat. The upper windows were rendered almost opaque because of fine lace curtains masking the view.

Faint sounds carried to Sam from the deserted rear of the saloon, the rear of which was opposite the big house. He rode on past, turned right along the perimeter of the holdings and gazed at the building from its west side, across the top of a border of shrubs.

More trees broke up the landscape to westward. The whole area seemed deserted. Sam dismounted. He went through the motions of checking the chestnut's shoes for the benefit of anyone unseen who might have him under observation. Still no cause for alarm. He lowered the last leg, pretended to notice for the first time the hitching rail beside the west gate to the property, and casually hitched the animal to it.

He hoped as he moved through the gate that it would look as if he was entering to ask for assistance. The rear verandah was hidden from the road by an end wall. As soon as he deemed himself to be out of view from passers by, he relaxed; mopped his head, face and brow with his green bandanna.

Signs of opulence in the way of furniture, curtains and so on, dimly seen through more lace drapes. No dogs, no reason to think himself observed. He knocked at the back door. No response. On round the garden side after trying the door handle. Windows but no doors. Another corner: the front verandah, the swing, creaking very slightly for want of oil. Another door, which he approached like a professional and then abandoned rather hurriedly. On his tour of the building, he had decided that he would definitely go indoors, even if he didn't touch anything in the interior.

Backtracking, he tested the blade of his knife on two windows. The catch on one of those at the rear gave easily. Up went the window. All he had to do was negotiate the sill. He glanced around, failed to notice anyone beyond the hitchrail, and decided to move in.

Just before he did so, he glanced up at the widespread branches of a tree growing at the corner of the rear lawn, the branches of which were scarcely clear of the window above him on the top floor. The first strong breeze would make the tip of the branch tap the window.

An adroit move and he was in. A sitting-room with the expensive furniture hidden in protecting covers. One or two landscape oil paintings on the walls. A big oval mirror on an inner wall. Also on the ground floor was a small hall, a kitchen, a dining room and a library.

Upstairs were three bedrooms and a bathroom, all tastefully furnished, but his eyes were on other things. He extended the spyglass he had brought with him. Now, he moved from window to window, giving all his attention to the out of doors. While he studied the views to the east, south and west he found himself wondering how long his fellow conspirators would expect him to be indoors.

Half an hour? One hour? Several hours, possibly, in a protracted search for hidden money. They had been vague. He was thinking that there were far too few people about for normal when he got his first sighting of one of his partners. Mayo had emerged from the saloon to sit on the rear gallery with a tall glass of beer in his hand and a cigar between his lips.

Mayo's attention was down the street, towards the east. So where was Gafferty? Towards the east, most probably, although he was invisible to Sam. Deliberately, Sam tweaked the curtain opposite Mayo. His move had an interesting reaction. Mayo took note of it, tapped his cigar three times in succession to remove the ash from it and casually stepped back into the shadowed interior of the saloon.

Sam kept out of sight after that from

the street, but he was down on one knee at another window, patiently looking for signs of Gafferty. He had read the signal given by Mayo, but what did it mean? Treachery of some sort . . . Suddenly Gafferty appeared. He was on foot, crossing from the avenue of cottonwoods towards the intersection by which Sam had arrived. Little Joe looked as if he had an urgent appointment and Sam, who was mightily suspicious, thought he knew where Gafferty was going. His route lay across North, into Main and up the street as far as the peace office.

Sam could guess at his words. *'Excuse me, marshal, I'm only a stranger in these parts, but jest now I seen the face of a man movin' around the windows of the bedrooms of that big house, Casablanca. Shucks, I could be wrong, but I had the impression the owners was away . . .'*

The marshal would do a double take, round up as many of his deputies as he could find and come running to protect the home of one of Indian Wells' most respected citizens. Unless Sam had badly miscalculated. He could have been wrong about his partners' treachery, but just a short time was all that was necessary to prove him right. Five to ten minutes, he decided, were his before the peace officers could get along to try and catch him on the job.

Gathering a little confidence, he lit a cigar before deliberately prowling the rooms again for signs of money hidden away. The safe turned up in the first room he had entered. It was not locked, and its contents consisted of early photographs and a few old family documents. No wads of money. Nothing behind the superb pictures which adorned the walls in most of the rooms. Gradually, his forward thinking cleared itself. Even if he had not been framed, he could not rob this household of its treasures just to improve his standing with outlaws.

He had just come to this decision when three gun shots echoed across the town from the direction Gafferty had taken. They were so spaced out that Sam was certain they had been fired to alert others, probably by the town marshal himself.

At the nearest upper window he peered anxiously down the street, hovering before making good his departure. His unaccountable reluctance to quit the building almost led to his undoing. Feet were pounding up from the North Street intersection when a loud raucous voice shouted from near the south-west corner of the building.

'Hurry it up, marshal! Somebody's in the house for sure! There's a horse hitched up the street, here!'

At this, Sam's throat went dry. The last thing he wanted to do was be caught in the house. Nor did he want to have to shoot his way out, firing against honest decent citizens. He began to wish he had not volunteered for this hazardous way of life, especially when his straining ears caught the peace officer's hoarse reply.

'Never mind about the horse, get in there! See if you can bust in the back door, an' don't forget what your shootin' iron's for!'

At the head of the stairs, Sam hesitated. He was casting around in his thoughts for another escape route when a bullet penetrated a panel of the back door and speeded his thinking. Fortunately, his head was clear. He raced into the rear bedroom where the tree branches were encroaching. As the back door was kicked in, he raised the window and leaned out. His first pursuer was indoors. No signs of others at the back.

He wiped his hands on his shirt, crouched on the sill for a few seconds and launched himself at the nearest branch. It held his weight without creaking and enabled him to make two frantic swings towards the bole. Then, he was on his way down. His shirt and vest suffered in the descent, but otherwise he was down unhurt.

He raced away from the tree towards the north, partially hidden by shrubs and wooden fencing. Breathing hard, he rounded a further fence beyond the lawn which hid the vegetable garden from the house and sprinted flat out towards the western boundary where the spirited chestnut awaited him.

The pursuers were exchanging breathless shouts around the house as he shook the reins loose and vaulted into the saddle. No shouts of recognition followed him as he rowelled his mount into a brisk trot away from the Casablanca and into the first of the scattering of trees and wayward shrubs which ringed the modest settlement. The chestnut responded well. He thought fleetingly of the man who had made him a present of it: of the men in Conchas City on whose behalf he was acting now.

Gafferty had said to bring the loot out to a spot some little distance north of the west trail out of town, to a rendezvous. Surely, on reflection, that advice was too vague for a proper rendezvous. No time stated, no suggestion of distance.

Sam rode on doggedly. He felt that he had been made a fool of: that he was lucky to get clear of the building in the way he had. That he had come out of this exercise with very low marks. His employers would never countenance what he had done. He was leaving town fleeing for his life for the first time in his life.

Maybe he had seen the last of the judge's enemies. He figured that they had made a fool of him, right from the start. They had never intended to profit by his entry into the deserted house. Such thoughts did little for his morale. One thing he was sure of, though. He had no intention of riding to the vague rendezvous west of town.

10

For half a mile, Sam kept north of the trail going west. In that time, he kept up a goodly pace and at the same time managed to get his emotions under control. He felt almost certain that his two partners had given him away to the town marshal, but he could not be one hundred per cent sure.

He knew that he had gambled in using the name of Colt Brogan, and that his gamble had been a very long shot. Maybe he would never know what their true thoughts were on the subject of Brogan. On the other hand, instead of taking him into town and betraying him they could quite well have shot him at the outset, when he first arrived at their isolated shack.

Instinct took him gradually nearer the west trail out of town although he had no idea at all of looking for

Gafferty and Mayo. He had a feeling that if the route was clear of pursuit, he ought to get on it and speed up his withdrawal from Indian Wells. In the last of a tree belt, he surveyed the track in both directions, decided that there were no indications at all of a posse, and moved into it with mild feelings of relief.

He felt for his canteen, tilted a few mouthfuls of water past his lips, mopped his head and neck with his bandanna and began something which he had so far put off. His plans for the future.

Was it out and away, and back to Conchas City to report a few frightening possibilities, but otherwise failure? Or out of the area altogether? Neither of these occurred to him as a serious possibility. What then? Should he head back into trouble, or steer round the edge of it? His general discomfort, largely due to perspiration and uncertainty, led him to scratch his back. He had a semi-permanent ache in the region of the backbone at belt level. Recollection of the cause of his discomfort made him smile. The pouch. Ever since he left Conchas City, he had had the leather pouch with the counterfeit notes in it. Brocius' spending money, left behind in Bridgetown.

Two thousand dollars worth of duds. Why had he brought it with him? He tried to remember his exact thoughts when he asked his employers to allow him to bring the bad notes with him. He could not clearly recollect why he had done so. While his mind wrestled with old motives, however, a new possibility occurred to him. He had been sent into the deserted house to collect money: a large sum of money.

Perhaps two thousand dollars might seem a large sum of money to Gafferty and his sidekick. Twenty home-made hundred dollar bills. Was it feasible, he wondered, to pass off to the outlaws the work of a counterfeiter? Would they accept it as cash brought from the house, Casablanca?

Having covered a couple of miles on

the proper track, he moved off it again on a downgrade, and still he had not made up his mind. Was a reunion with the outlaws really worth the risk? After a lot of worrying conjecture, a mental image of Melissa Sherman in her strolling outfit helped to make up his mind. He recollected that she had once had a young brother, and that although he had won the confidence of her father he had not had the chance to get to know her at all.

Should a man risk his life for a girl he had seen but once in his travels? Most men would say it was a foolish reason, but no one really needed to be told. Somehow he had to make her change her mind about him, as her father had done. And so it was that he put aside his doubts, and headed quite definitely for the rendezvous shack.

★　★　★

Due to detours, the ride back was more punishing than the one into town. It was turned nine o'clock in the evening as he approached it with his mind full of explanations and telling words to use on Gafferty and Mayo. He felt certain that he was ahead of them, but it was as well to have his mind clear on certain points.

His first surprise was the smoke swirling up from the pipe above the stove. His second came when he noticed two horses which were not those on which his partners had ridden into town. The third came with his recognition of a big grey horse, the hide of which was liberally marked with black spots.

How could he ever forget that particular horse? It was one of the three he had been asked to choose between on the occasion when he had acquired the chestnut.

★   ★   ★

In the shack, there was also speculation. Hank Weldon was scratching nervously at his neat grey beard as he watched the approach of the young man who had acquired his chestnut horse. He pulled off his big black hat and ran his hand over his shaven skull.

'Hey, Doc, come on over here an' take a look at this young fellow approachin'!'

Doc Danton was a tall thin man of forty with bulbous dead-pan eyes. He was smartly dressed in a black flat-crowned stetson and a cutaway coat of the same colour. His cranial hair was long, brown and wavy and extended down the sides of his jaw in long side-burns. Under the coat he wore a white shirt, a string tie and a grey double-breasted waistcoat which matched the colour of his tailored trousers.

As he ghosted across the shack to the window where Weldon was, his long wrists came out of his sleeve ends and brushed back his coat to reveal a pair of twin .44s slung low either side of his body. His expression was a wolfish frown, which showed a good set of teeth in a pallid face.

His voice was pitched low in timbre. 'Trouble?'

In a few glib sentences, Weldon explained how Gould had turned up at the ranch unexpectedly, how he had left with the chestnut, and where the black he sought had come from.

'You think he had reason to go after Jake Mayo for revenge?'

'Like I said before . . . or did I? Maybe I jest thought it. I don't rightly know. He left the Circle W in good spirits an' I would have thought he had gone back to wherever he came from without lookin' for Jake any more.'

Danton said: 'Sure does seem strange, him ridin' up to the one shack where he can be sure of locatin' Mayo. He's comin' along like he's been here before.'

By this time, Sam had dismounted. The time allowed for preliminary conjecture was almost over. Weldon had the opportunity to suggest that he — Weldon — should take the initiative, and then Sam was approaching and the rancher was heading for the door. As it opened, they met, and the expression on the rancher's face almost matched that of the redhead for surprise. Neither of them, in fact, was showing what he really felt.

'Why, Sam! Sam Gould, of all people. I don't rightly know why, but I never thought to see you in this neck of the woods. Come on right in an' take the weight offen your legs. This here is an associate of mine, Doc Danton. Doc, meet Sam Gould. Sit down, why don't you?'

To cover his embarrassment and the excitement which was building inside him, Sam fished out three small cigars. He apologized for the small amount of tobacco which had spilled out of them and offered one each to the other two. Danton, who had briefly shaken his hand, rasped a match on a thumb nail with a movement like a sleight of hand conjuror and studied Sam's face in close-up through the flame.

When they were all seated and

smoking, Weldon pushed the conversation along a little. 'Tell me, Sam, ain't you a little ways off your regular route out here in the outback? Jest for a few seconds before you came in, the Doc an' me, we thought you looked as if you'd been here before.'

Sam mopped his neck with his bandanna, shrugged easily and grinned. 'It's a fair question, Mr Weldon. I have been here before. As a matter I've been on a job of sorts for a couple of friends, a sort of a trial job in Indian Wells. I could tell you more about it, but maybe my friends would think I'd been indiscreet.'

Weldon waved his cigar. 'Tactfully put, my young friend. I understand perfectly. But if the two hombres you have in mind happen to be called Joe and Jake, you don't have to hold back because I know them a whole lot better than you do. Ain't it a small world now?'

The rancher started to laugh. His rounded figure shook. His mirth sounded genuine. Sam joined in, but his green eyes never missed anything. He was intrigued by the way in which Doc Danton smiled broadly without betraying the slightest feeling. Danton was the first to detect the sounds of further arrivals.

'All right, we can have a glorious reunion in a few minutes,' he murmured. 'Jake an' Little Joe are on the way in.'

Sam's mind was churning with ideas. If Hank Weldon was willing to confess his close association with Little Joe and Jake Mayo, that had to mean something. Perhaps he had made a bold and telling move in returning to this shack after his period of indecision. All differences could be settled, or he could be eliminated as a result of this coming reunion.

Weldon yelled for the others to enter. Mayo and Gafferty had been warned what to expect, having seen the giveaway chestnut and the big spotted grey. Little Joe grinned and sniffed, and eyed all three men already in the cabin before crossing to a shelf and lifting down a whisky bottle. Mayo called a general greeting and lowered his length onto a low bunk, his teeth chewing on a matchstick.

Sam had time to notice that both Mayo and Gafferty were more surprised and curious about the presence of Doc Danton than they were of himself. Clearly they were wary of the tall gunman and they acted as though he was a stranger to them.

The redhead accepted his drink in a chipped mug without protest. He drank about half his measure while the others were similarly engaged. He was keen to clarify his own position as early as possible, and this prompted him to speak out.

'Well, boys, you'll be glad to know my one-man raid on the house known as Casablanca was a success, in spite of the fact that the peace officers got wind of my entry.'

He slipped out of his vest and

removed the leather pouch from the back of his waistband, tossing it on the table, where Weldon reached for it, opened it up and hauled out the bills. Sam murmured the amount. The rancher checked it and nodded, glancing up at Joe and Jake for any observations.

'So you sent Sam on a trial job into Indian Wells, Joe? That seems reasonable. An' now he's come up with two thousand dollars for the funds. Are you satisfied with him?'

Before either of them could comment, Sam remarked: 'I had the opinion they doubted me before I went. I'd like to feel all their doubts are removed now, Mr Weldon, before we embark on a closer association.'

Weldon nodded and waited for Joe's reaction, which was slow in coming. 'We were a little doubtful because we had heard from other sources that Colt Brogan had died in South America. Right now, though, I don't suppose it matters. Gould has made a good start.

He ducked out an' got clear away without any assistance from us. Are you goin' to tell him what your special plans are?'

Weldon rolled his cigar round the side of his mouth, spat out a sliver of tobacco and drained his glass. 'Reckon I am at that, Joe. Doc Danton, here, Sam, is the newest man on my payroll. He's joined us to help with a certain plan, the elimination of an old enemy. A man who's dropped out of the limelight these days. I speak of Judge H. Dan Sherman, now residing on ranchland south of West Flats.'

11

Although all parties were desperately keen to know Weldon's plans for furthering the campaign against his hated enemy, Judge Sherman, the liquor and the need to eat cut short talk about the future, and effectively postponed it until the following morning.

Weldon slept in the loft. Gafferty and Mayo shared a pair of bunks, and Sam found himself sleeping on the bunk above Doc Danton who coughed from time to time in the night as though he had a touch of lung trouble. Getting off to sleep was not an easy exercise for Sam. He kept marvelling over the fact that he was accepted as a conspirator with a bunch coldly dedicated to eliminating his employer. Until this day, his work and what lay behind it had seemed divorced from reality. Now, he had to believe everything and he was

171

likely to be in the thick of the action.

After breakfast, provided by Gafferty and Mayo, who rose at an early hour, Weldon called his team to order and outlined his immediate plans.

'The day after tomorrow, there is a sort of fete day in Conchas Cty. Accordin' to what I'm able to find out, the judge ain't likely to show himself around the stalls 'cause he don't like crowds, but that daughter of his, Melissa, she's different again. Ain't nothin' will keep her away.'

Melissa's beauty was known to all present except Danton, and even he betrayed an interest when he went to work on his nails with the point of his knife blade. Sam studied the eyes of the plotters. Danton's were like bullet tips. Mayo's resembled blue stones, while those of Gafferty seemed to grow closer together. It was Weldon's pair of near-black eyes, however, which easily dominated the others. The young redhead looked away. He did not like the revelation about the interest in

Melissa, and yet he dared not let anyone know his true feelings.

Gafferty broke the silence. 'You thinkin' of another kidnap, Boss?'

Weldon nodded. He eyed them in turn, Sam last. His cheroot was pointed at the redhead when he started to explain. 'Sam, here, spent a short while in Conchas, but he has no reason to like the Shermans. In fact, we know the judge stopped him from doin' legitimate business by havin' the machinery smashed when he wanted to start up the newspaper. I'm thinkin' of havin' Sam lure the Sherman girl into our clutches. You other three could be ready to grab her when he gets her to a suitable spot. Take a cart, with a canopy over, of course.

'Think you could get the girl away from her chaperone, Sam, or would that be too difficult?'

Sam nodded slightly to show that he was weighing up the suggestion. He was thinking that he would not be in a strong position to help the girl in the event that the three killers took the initiative.

'It could be very difficult in crowds, Mr Weldon, but I'm willin' to have a go, if that's what you want. When do we start?'

'I knew you'd agree, boy. I like your style. Now, off you go an' get the horses groomed. I've one or two more instructions to give these other hombres, an' I want you all on your way in an hour.'

Sam complied with his instructions. He was too smart to try and hang about close enough to hear what followed. The rest wandered out and joined him by the hollow where the horses were pegged out some fifteen minutes later. Weldon handed out twenty dollars apiece for expenses, heaved his bulk into the saddle of the grey, which was all ready for the trail, and went off on his own with scarcely a backward glance.

Five minutes later, the quartette of riders left. Gafferty and Mayo kept about twenty yards ahead during most of that day. Sam came next, and the wary loner, Doc Danton, brought up the rear. Their route lay south. They crossed the Bridgetown-West Flats trail, broke for a meal around noon, and carried on across untrailed country in a south-easterly direction until early evening. Their night campfire was more than half way towards Conchas.

After the meal, Mayo made one or two lighthearted efforts to draw Danton into their conversation, but the responses were guarded and lacked warmth. As they went off to sleep, wrapped in their blankets, Sam found himself wondering if Weldon had brought in Danton as a sort of watchdog over Gafferty and Mayo, and the latter pair had ideas along the same lines. Danton had a reputation as a top hired gun in other parts, and they knew it.

Shortly before dawn, Little Joe and his partner clattered on a frying pan and prompted an early start. The meal was slightly hurried, and the reason for the haste soon became apparent. Joe and Jake were going off on their own to collect a covered wagon from a sympathetic party not many miles away.

Danton and Sam waited beside the Bridgetown-Conchas trail until the four-horse conveyance with its green canvas patched in places rolled up to meet them around eleven a.m. For a short while, they pulled off-trail and took coffee, talking over what they had to do when they reached town. After that, the outlaws went to some trouble not to attract attention from the many travellers using the route to the busy town.

Sam took a turn on the box of the wagon while Danton reclined in the back, his skewbald trotting along behind the tailgate. The other pair had dropped back a good hundred yards, and were prepared to ride off-trail for a while rather than be studied by curious travellers.

Later on, the roles were reversed.

Sam had a short rest on the mattress, but when they finally struck the northern outskirts of town and looked for an isolated patch on which to pitch a tent, he was forking the chestnut and nearly a furlong behind.

After their evening meal, they strolled into town and saw where the stalls and enclosures had been rigged for the events of the following day. Inevitably, Sam's thoughts were troubled ones. One or other of the trio was always with him. He had no opportunity to slip away and warn his friends of the kidnap plot for the following day.

Consequently, he slept badly.

★ ★ ★

It was a little after eleven the following morning when Sam first caught sight of Melissa Sherman in the crowded Main Street of the town. With his heart thumping, he hitched the chestnut to a rail at the corner of an intersection, and carried on on foot after the pretty girl

177

and her female chaperone.

He knew that if he did not approach the girl as he had been instructed the ruthless trio he had entered town with would take direct action, and that his own future safety would be in jeopardy. He kept about twenty yards behind them through the milling crowds, hoping against hope that an opportunity would present itself for him to spirit the girl out of danger.

The chaperone was a greying brunette in her middle forties wearing a pale blue dress and matching bonnet under a parasol. In the hand which held the parasol, the woman had another item. It looked like a rattle. Sam guessed that she would raise the alarm with it in the event of a threat to Melissa.

Ahead of them was a tall conical tent. The strollers had to push away from it to avoid tripping over the guy ropes. Melissa and her escort, the widow Pilson, stepped up onto the sidewalk to get out of the crush. It was clear to Sam that Melissa was interested in the fortune-teller who was using the tent.

While he was hovering about below the sidewalk rail with his hat pulled low, there was a diversion. The fortune teller, a woman of mature years whose skin suggested either Indian or gypsy blood, emerged from the tent and hung a big sign on the flap which informed the strollers that she would be away for a half hour.

There were a few catcalls as disappointed visitors moved away again, but the fortune teller took no notice, merely tossing her head and making the metal baubles jingle on the head scarf which covered it. Wrapping her black shawl around her more tightly, she pushed away from the tent, yelling imprecations in what sounded like Spanish.

Sam acted upon impulse, making up his mind to take advantage of the woman's absence. He forced his way further along the dirt road, only pausing when he was directly below the two women. After peering around to make sure he was not overheard, he raised his voice.

'Miss Sherman!'

He raised his hat briefly so that the two females could take a good look at him. He knew his voice had reached them because they both gasped, and the sharp featured little chaperone shifted the rattle from one hand to the other.

'I'm Sam Gould. I've been workin' for your Pa out of town. Right now there's trouble. Your Pa's enemies are in town seekin' to kidnap you. I want you to trust me. Touch your hat if you understand.'

A long ten seconds elapsed before the startled pink-cheeked brunette complied. Sam sighed with relief. He found time to think how well her blue two-piece outfit suited her along with the straw bonnet enlivened with blue ribbon.

'I'm goin' to try an' get into that tent from the back, unobserved. Give me two or three minutes and then make your way in through the ordinary flap.

I'll be waitin' for you. Have your escort wait right here in case she's needed.'

There was a short sharp clash of wills up there on the sidewalk before the judge's daughter gained the upper hand. Sam averted his gaze, touched his hat and started to push through the crowd. Shortly afterwards, he contrived to drop a handful of small coins on the ground behind the tent. One or two sharp-movers picked up a couple, but nothing impeded him as he crawled under the canvas to recover a silver dollar which he claimed had rolled that way.

As he straightened up in the narrow confines of the tent, the trapped heat brought him out in perspiration. He glanced around it, frowning uncomfortably and began to take in its contents. In the middle was a square solid table with its legs embedded in the dirt. On the table was a glass of the type known as a crystal ball, two packs of cards, a tea cup and a big square cloth with Indian designs on it. Hanging suspended from the wall was a big-brimmed steeple hat and a multi-coloured poncho with a brown fringe.

He was surprised when Melissa lifted the flap, stepped swiftly inside and confronted him. He whipped off his hat, tried to reassure her by his expression, and failed. His eyes reflected his great interest as she took off her bonnet and used it to fan herself.

She tossed back her black bell of hair, smiled nervously at first and then more becomingly. Her wide blue eyes searched his face for the first time in close-up. He found the sensation quite captivating.

'Well, Mr Sam Gould, what plans do you have to prevent my bein' kidnapped?'

Her voice was nicely modulated, and yet it showed a trace of her nervousness.

He started off: 'It's no joke, Miss Sherman. Your Pa knows full well who his enemies are an' what they are likely to attempt. I have to appear to still be co-operatin' with them — '

'Please don't waste time on further explanation. I trust you. What do you want me to do?'

Sam licked his dry lips and swallowed hard. 'I want you to take off that skirt, and get into that poncho and sombrero. I have a key to the old *Clarion* office. You must hide there until the men who came with me are safely out of town.'

Melissa's face coloured up momentarily with anger, but her eyes stopped flashing almost as soon as they had started. She turned her back on him and began to take off the skirt. Chuckling to hide her embarrassment, she murmured: 'I guess if anyone looked in now you might get yourself lynched for rape or something.'

Sam's sense of humour, however, had gone back on him. 'Hm, I hadn't thought of that. The chances are I'll die of lead poisonin' before I've finished doin' this undercover job for your father.'

She turned sharply, and divined his

true feelings behind the forced smile. 'I shouldn't have said that, Sam, even in fun. I'm sorry. I — I hope you'll live for many years yet an' feel the need to know us a whole lot better.'

'Mighty nice of you to say so, Miss Melissa. Kind of puts a different complexion on things when you say that. Here, I'll hold the poncho for you. It ain't as clean as I would have wanted, but I guess it'll have to do.'

The sombrero hid most of her head, and the poncho corners trailed the floor. He felt like a shop-lifter as he lifted the hat for one close look into her face, but he was rewarded by a brief kiss on the lips which acted as a mild shock.

He pushed the key into her hand. 'Send your chaperone to look for the town marshal. The kidnappers are three men who came along with a covered wagon. You must go straight to that office an' stay there.'

'I promise, Sam.' The look in her eyes held promise of a different type, and then she was gone.

12

A brief current of warm air, and then he was alone with only the slight movement near the opening to remind him that Melissa had been there, and that she had put herself in his hands. He glanced down at his hands, suddenly concerned as to whether they had been clean or not. He noticed that they trembled a little.

It was not just the excitement of that all too brief interlude with her. Mostly it was fear for her future. She was out there and moving with the crowd up the street. If any of his so-called partners had noticed his unorthodox entrance to the tent, and the way in which the girl had barged in disregarding the 'Back in a half hour' notice, then he and she could be in trouble.

He stepped to the opening and cautiously lifted the flap. He saw enough to know that the chaperone woman had moved away. The crowd was still as numerous. The approach of lunch time had done nothing to thin out the sightseers.

What now?

If Melissa's disguise had been seen through, he was not in a position to help. She had already gone. Although maybe only a hundred yards separated them, he might just as well have been a hundred miles away. He rested a hip on the table, lit a small cigar and further added to the unpleasantness of the atmosphere.

When he had last seen Little Joe, Jake Mayo and Doc Danton, they had been hovering fairly close to the covered wagon which had been moved into the street further north and abandoned there with its horse team still in the shafts.

Now, he found himself wondering if one or other of them had followed him when he took off on his own. The chances were that they had. But they might not have noticed how he had ducked into the tent. Melissa's entrance could have been visible to anyone close, but he took comfort from the fact that the outlaws might not know exactly what she looked like.

If one of them had guessed that he was up to something, he would probably have a visit in the tent before the fortune-teller returned. He gave himself as long as his cigar lasted before emerging into the street and mingling with the crowd.

Perhaps he ought to get back to the others, in the event that no one approached him. His nerves played him up, as he sucked hard on the cigar. A body barged against the tent wall, but it was only a stumble. With half an inch unsmoked, he gave up. It was time to go.

He tossed it in the dirt, stuck his boot over it and suddenly the person he least expected to see was in there with him. The fortune-teller had returned early, smelling strongly of whisky.

He stepped back, smiled, and started to explain but her sharp eyes had noticed that the poncho and sombrero were missing. He put two dollar pieces on the table without managing to stem the woman's sudden outburst of temper.

She raised her voice, roundly cursed him in Spanish, called him a thief and an intruder and swung at him with her twisted shawl.

Sam dodged round the table, pushed her aside and lunged for the entrance. He was almost through it when she extended her long leg and tripped him. He pitched forward into the sun-bright packed street and sprawled on all fours through the legs of the nearest passers-by. His hat came off. Jostled sightseers called out in alarm. He grabbed for his hat, got a grip on it and caused a woman to scream as his shoulder collided with her legs.

Someone sprawled across his back. Others came down. He crawled on, aiming blindly for the sidewalk. In the background, the fortune-teller had scrambled up on a wooden crate and was loudly shouting about the intruder and beseeching passing men to get a hold on him.

The nearest people noticed him as he straightened up in their midst. He shouldered his way to the sidewalk, scrambled up onto it and was at once seen by the gypsy woman. He ran in the direction of the intersection where he had left his horse.

In his haste, he overturned a basket on the arm of a plump woman, spilling foodstuffs and souvenirs which she had just purchased. Her husband, a burly farmer, gave chase. Sam jumped down into the dirt again, removed his hat once more and pushed for all he was worth.

As he broke clear of the packed groups and lunged for his horse, someone behind him swung a hand rattle. He had not time to find out if it was Melissa's chaperone or someone else making the noise on account of the trail of suspicion, ill-feeling and down-right anger which pursued him.

With the leather of the saddle under him, he felt slightly more at ease, but within a minute a bunch of horsemen came down the intersection, clearly following him, and headed by a deputy town marshal on a big roan horse. Sam headed south. He kept ahead of them by zigzagging when the opportunity presented itself. He used deserted alleyways and the open spaces provided by vacant lots. Soon, the posse was strung out. He turned west with only the deputy distantly at his back, luckily shook him off when the latter's horse collided with a fruit stall. The fruit went in all directions. The peace officer's horse panicked and threw him. Sam gained a few more yards.

In another street, he dismounted and attempted to blend in with the scene. Nearing the west end of town, he mounted up again, and diverged through trees until he struck the trail north. His spirits were low as he headed out of town. If Melissa had been taken he had no means of knowing.

If she was in safety, then he had done some good. But he did not relish facing Weldon with an elaborate set of excuses, this time about the failure of the kidnap.

*   *   *

In spite of the sensation caused by Sam and the fortune-teller, the day of fete continued to be a success. Two hours after the incident Melissa was rescued from the *Clarion* office by Marshal Stevens, who had retrieved her skirt. She was taken along with her chaperone to the hotel, and there put in a private sitting room, guarded by the marshal himself and Walter Vilman who had been informed as to what was taking place.

A couple of part-time constables came to report to the marshal shortly afterwards. They had been given the task of keeping watch on the covered wagon which had been standing abandoned in the street to the north for so long.

The senior of the two was a tall man with a sprouting grey moustache who carried a shotgun. He removed his straight-brimmed dented-crowned Scout hat and reported.

'Marshal, we've left Briggs still keepin' watch on that wagon, but so far no one has been near it. It begins to look as if the men who brought it into town have abandoned it.'

Stevens glared at the lawyer before answering them. 'All right. But keep patrollin' you two, on account of that trio may still be in town. Anythin' suspicious, get in touch right away. Fire off your gun if you want help in a hurry.'

As soon as they had gone about their business, the marshal turned to Vilman who was sharing a table with him near the door.

'I don't like it, Walter. I don't like it at all. That young redhead, Gould, is no doubt tryin' hard but he doesn't have the experience. He approached Miss Melissa, here, an' that act alone could have plunged her into danger. The very danger we seek to avoid.'

'Of course we don't know what pressure he was under, Pete, but I can understand your concern. If I'd been in his shoes, I'd have made contact with the peace office before makin' any sort of positive move.'

Vilman sounded mild, but he was troubled, too. His baggy grey eyes were scarcely ever still. He turned and glanced towards Melissa and the older woman and got a mixed reception. The girl hurriedly glanced away, while Mrs Pilson transformed her sharp features by a sweet smile of approval. Vilman held his thick cigar with his elbow planted on the table, as though the tobacco were heavy.

The girl murmured: 'If it hadn't been for Sam Gould, I might now be on my way out of town, trussed up in the back of a covered wagon, and none of you would have been any the wiser.'

'What's this about bein' trussed in a covered wagon, my girl?'

Judge Sherman, who had come into

town for the express purpose of collecting his daughter and taking her back to the ranch, pushed the door further open and stepped inside. Mrs Pilson came to her feet and did a little bow. Sherman crossed over to his daughter, who threw herself into his arms and placed her head on his chest.

The judge hugged her, but his troubled eyes were asking questions of the other two men present. Vilman and Stevens both started to explain together. They checked themselves, and while Sherman was disengaging himself and taking a chair beside his daughter, the two men moved closer.

Melissa said: 'The troubles have started again, Pa. I think you knew an' you didn't tell me. I'm grown up now an' I have a right to know.'

Sherman nodded and stroked her hair. The males seemed to be suddenly embarrassed and presently the girl began a graphic description of what had happened to her since Sam Gould made his furtive approach in front of the fortune-teller's tent.

She spoke well of Sam, and her eyes betrayed her intense interest in the young man as she talked. Sherman noticed this. Some of the edge was taken off his forebodings by it, and the weight around his heart eased slightly as he realized that the day might very well have been calamitous for them.

'Whatever we do, gentlemen, we must not underestimate Sam Gould,' Sherman remarked thoughtfully. 'It's my opinion he couldn't contact us because he was watched most of the time. We must keep up our vigilance, keep lookin' for those three men an' have a constant watch kept on the vehicle we think they planned to use.

'As for Melissa an' me, we'll be stayin' in the hotel tonight. I wouldn't relish ridin' back to the ranch this evenin' after what has happened.'

All the tension went out of the girl as she heard this suggestion about staying in town. She soon looked glum again, however, when the judge made it clear that she would be staying indoors for the rest of the day. For her, sightseeing was over until another fete.

13

A haze of blue tobacco smoke hung about the rafters and ceiling of the Weldon rendezvous shack at three o'clock in the afternoon, two days later. The rancher himself was sitting at the table with his legs sprawled out and his brow furrowed with wrinkles of concentration as he strove to work out a hand of patience.

Sam's plodding horse broke in upon his concentration at the full extent of earshot. At once, Weldon stiffened. He had received no information about the outcome of the plot. His nerves were keyed up and his tuft of chin beard moved up and down as he gnawed his underlip and rocked back and forth on his chair.

Even without looking through the window, he had worked out who the solitary horseman was and also what the news was likely to be. His astute mind was putting theories to the test which would fit the circumstances of one of his men returning without the others.

Sam was dismounting when the rancher called to him.

'Come on indoors, Sam, an' give me all the news! You must be near on tuckered out by your efforts in gettin' back here this soon!'

'I figured you'd want to know what went on as soon as possible, so I kept right on pushin' it. I'm afraid the news is bad.'

Weldon's mouth and teeth clenched afresh round his cigar. He gestured for Sam to take a seat on the other side of the table and pushed a whisky bottle towards him. The latter poured for himself, swished a mouthful around his tongue and swallowed it.

The tone of Weldon's voice had changed when he said: 'Smoke?'

Sam accepted a cigar. He began his explanation as soon as it was lit, having discarded his sweat-stained hat. 'I don't know quite what happened to the other three, Mr Weldon. I separated from them an' got on the track of the Sherman girl around eleven in the mornin'. For quite a time, I didn't have any idea how to get her away from the chaperone woman, or how to arrange for her to leave the crowds.

'Then I spotted a fortune-teller's tent. The girl was mighty keen to have her palm read, or somethin', so I slipped into the tent while the gypsy woman was out. I knew the Sherman girl wouldn't go far. But it didn't work out the way I wanted. You see, the fortune-teller came back earlier than was expected, reekin' of whisky an' she caused a stir, all right.

'Accused me of robbin' her of some clothes, an' wanted me put in a cell. However, I managed to scramble away through the crowds an' mount up. After that, a bunch of riders came after me headed by a deputy, so I took them on a circular tour, gave them the slip and kept on out of town.'

Weldon picked up the pack of cards. He squared them up, flicked the set from one hand to the other and spat his cigar out.

'All right, that'll do for now, Sam. The others will come back when they're good an' ready. Get yourself a bite to eat, clean up a bit an' turn in for a while. Me, I'm goin' for a stroll. Don't worry about a thing.'

So saying, Hank Weldon stood up, shrugged his shoulders and walked out of the building, planting his feet heavily at every step. No power on earth would have prevented Sam from worrying. Somehow, in spite of the tension which had to build up before the return of the outlaw trio, he managed to take the other's advice. Having washed and eaten and taken care of the chestnut, he turned in on a low bunk and to his surprise later, dropped off to sleep almost at once.

★　★　★

To Hank Weldon his operatives were expendable. Nevertheless, in the special case of Little Joe Gafferty and Jake Mayo who, along with the new man, Doc Danton, knew his mind on the subject of Judge Sherman, he felt some concern. Over the years, he had employed many men who lived by the gun and it was his experience that they did not always get on well together.

Consequently, when he spotted the trio with the aid of his spyglass shortly after five o'clock that same afternoon, he felt a certain relief. He noted that Little Joe and Jake were riding together and that Danton was maintaining a discreet distance behind them.

Clearly, the kidnap plan had come to nothing. He felt bitter about that, although he had a few new ideas which could make for a sure success when a few tricky details were straightened out.

Weldon stood up on the bluff where he had been on lookout. He took a small round mirror from his pocket and so reflected the rays of the sun with it that almost at once Gafferty and Mayo reacted. Ten minutes later, the riders were up with him. The first two swung out of leather and walked forward, while Danton crooked a leg round his saddle horn and relaxed in his own particular fashion.

Joe said: 'Howdy, Boss. You must have been worried.'

'Howdy, boys. Glad you got back all right. I'm not so much worried as frustrated. You see, young Gould is already back. Seems he made an effort to decoy Sherman's daughter by a fortune-teller's tent, but his scheme was spoiled because the palmist or whatever she was came back early and drunk an' raised an unholy row. Where were you at the time?'

Danton cleared his throat: 'I was further up Main Street, the west end.' He inclined his head towards the other two.

Mayo remarked: 'Joe an' me, we was covering the east end of Main an' the intersections at that end.'

'Do you three have any notions about Gould's scheme an' what happened after?'

Gafferty sniffed as he dabbed his jowl with a damp bandanna. 'I was surprised that he came all this way on his own. Didn't expect him to make it before us, either. I reckon he wanted to get his explanation in first, Boss.'

'We can't say if his scheme was a good one, Boss,' Mayo put in thoughtfully, as he finger-combed his thick fair hair. 'If he hadn't led the deputy an' the posse all round the town and away, I'd have been suspicious of him.'

'Why were you suspicious, Jake?' Weldon queried icily.

'Because after the uproar, we noticed a watch was bein' kept on the covered wagon,' Danton explained, in his customary low measured tones. 'Somehow the peace officers got a line on the wagon. If we had gone back to it I reckon we would have been picked up.'

Finally, Danton dismounted and did a few knees bend exercises, while

Weldon's probing roving eyes surveyed them, one after the other.

'We go along with what Doc says, Boss,' Gafferty added. 'That was why we had to leave the wagon right where it was, an' come on out without it. You'd be suspicious of Gould, under the circumstances.'

Weldon nodded slowly and carefully, and went through the motions of crackling a cigar between his fingers. Having lit it, he appeared to be satisfied with what he had heard.

'Don't worry about the wagon, boys. As for the peace officers keepin' watch on it, there could be another explanation. Somebody earlier might have recognized a face. A likeness off a reward notice.'

At this suggestion, all three outlaws tensed up, eyed one another and writhed with anger they dared not show openly to their Boss. Weldon cackled in sudden delight at their discomfiture.

'Don't fret yourselves, boys, it was jest a notion. Besides, I've had some more information while you've been away. Maybe we can float a better scheme in a few days' time. Get yourselves back to the shack. Do what you have to do to relax. I'll be back there shortly.'

The trail-weary riders did not require any second telling to mount up and finish their protracted journey.

*   *   *

After the evening meal, the five men played cards. Weldon was content for Gafferty and Danton to win a few dollars, although he made sure that he won the last game before he announced that he was tired of playing. Around eight o'clock, the rancher became thoughtful and the others knew that he wanted to talk about the future.

'Next week, there's a law convention bein' held in the court house of Silver Springs, boys. A good many men in the legal profession will be there from this territory, Arizona, an' maybe the states to the north and east.'

From time to time since his return, Sam had found his thoughts straying to Melissa Sherman and the way she had trusted him. Although he had not had a lot of experience with women, he knew that he was strongly attracted to her: that because of his feeling for her he would contemplate taking risks on her father's behalf which would have seemed foolhardy when he first agreed to work for the judge.

Now, his mind was keyed up again. If he managed to thwart the judge's enemies and perhaps bring them to judgement for their crimes Sherman was bound to think well of him and he would have a chance to further his acquaintance with the girl.

'Any chance of the judge goin' to the convention, Mr Weldon?' he asked thoughtfully.

The trio of outlaws eyed him speculatively. They were keen to know the answer to his question. Weldon mopped his clean-shaven skull with a handkerchief. His black eyes were flashing when he answered.

'The judge will certainly get an invitation, but whether he will go or not is another matter. My own view is that he will decline. On account of his native caution, an' recent happenings in Conchas.

'If we are to make use of this information, we have to think of a way to entice him. A way to make sure that he will go to Silver Springs, an' thus give us a chance to get at him away from his home town.'

Weldon did not ask the obvious question. Instead, he studied the faces of his men, wondering what was going on in their heads. Sam thought he knew a way of prompting the judge to take up the invitation, but for a time he kept his idea to himself, knowing that if the judge did go to Silver Springs he could be eliminated. Gafferty murmured a few words about an idea which was soon shown to be impracticable. Mayo and Danton averted their eyes, feeling embarrassed because they did not have the mental make-up for the sort of scheme Weldon wanted. Besides, if their suggestions went wrong they knew they might be eliminated themselves by an irate Boss.

Weldon eventually prompted Sam. 'I think you must have a notion, Sam. Let's hear about it whatever it is. After all, your last little caper might well have payed off.'

'All right, I'll tell you,' the redhead conceded. 'When I was fishin' about among some papers in the *Clarion* office, I came across a telegraph message written in code. I managed to decipher it. It came from Grout, the dead man, an' it said that Little Joe Gafferty was free again.'

Little Joe coughed on tobacco smoke. His eyes rounded with surprise before his expression turned mean again. He muttered an oath, but Weldon silenced him in his keenness to hear more.

'Go ahead, Sam. You're interestin' us.'

'Well, I was thinkin' that if the judge received a message in the same code urgin' him to go to the law convention, that might jest do the trick. That way he might be lured into leavin' home. I believe I can remember the code well enough to concoct a message.'

Danton pointed a sharp forefinger in Sam's direction. 'How do you know the judge would be able to decipher it, Gould?'

Sam shrugged uneasily, knowing he had to be careful what he said.

'I don't rightly know if he could, Doc. But he's a pretty smart hombre, ain't he?'

'He is that,' Weldon agreed readily enough, 'otherwise he would have been buzzard bait long before now. Even though Grout is dead, I think a suitably worded coded message might draw him.'

Sam grinned nervously. 'Sure. We could give him the impression that it was put together by another Pinkerton operative, I think.'

'Okay, okay,' Weldon approved enthusiastically, 'we'll do it. Cyrus P. Quill, the county attorney, will be sendin' out the ordinary invitation, but we'll leave him out of it and do as you say. There's some paper over on that shelf, Sam. Start composin' it right away. Choose your words well. Meantime, me an' the boys will be studyin' a plan of the centre of Silver Springs, the courthouse an' such.'

Sam collected the paper and the pencil, but he was slow to compose the composition, as his ears were intent upon what was being said by the others.

Weldon began: 'Now, boys, as you know, Silver Springs is the county town in these parts. Located northeast of Bridgetown and Indian Wells. The courthouse is like this.'

The rancher started to sketch out a plan. With an effort, Sam worked on the message. He wrote:

Imperative you attend the law convention to make an important contact.

Then he reversed the message and patiently made the necessary adjustments to the vowels.

14

The weather remained baking hot. In the county of Conchas there did not seem to be much in the way of change: nothing to suggest that a most audacious attack was about to be made upon the life of one of the territory's best known legal men.

However, certain preliminaries did take place. The county attorney, acting as secretary for the important legal body promoting the law convention, sent out his invitations to all and sundry. Those who lived a long distance away were given plenty of time in which to make their preparations for the trip, but men in the same county had to make do with seven to ten days' notice.

That was the way it was with Judge Sherman, who used Conchas City as his base, a town scarcely two days' travel from the county seat and courthouse. By mid-morning on the Monday following the plotters' meeting, H. Dan Sherman was seated in the office of his friend and adviser, Walter Vilman.

Sherman was humming to himself as he paused in his letter-writing labours to put a better point on the tip of his pen. Having tried out the new point in the ink, he gazed absently for about a minute at the wall and thought about the man to whom he was writing.

While he was thinking, there was a polite knock on the glass of the door and the stooping bespectacled clerk came in. Sherman peered at him over his half-glasses and raised his brows.

'Judge, there's a message you might want to read before you finish your letter. Mr Vilman will be back shortly. He asked me to bring in this telegraph without waitin' for his return. It's difficult for an ordinary person to understand, but I believe you know something about readin' cryptic messages. I'll leave it with you, sir.'

At the mention of cryptic messages, the former judge's interest quickened. He took the sheet of paper, forgot to thank the clerk and at once pored over it. He appropriated a sheet of writing paper from the lawyer's desk and at once set about solving the coded message.

He had been busy for nearly a quarter of an hour when Vilman returned from a visit to the other side of town and joined him.

'What was it about, Dan? I mean the message that came by telegraph, of course. You haven't solved it already?'

Sherman nodded and chuckled in a rather tight-lipped fashion, indicating the solution to the message waiting for the lawyer on his blotting pad. Vilman hurriedly discarded his hat and moved behind the desk. Secretly, he was disappointed that the judge had managed to arrive at the solution before he — Vilman — got back.

He read: 'Imperative you attend the law convention to make an important contact.'

Sherman said: 'How about that, then, Walter? I must admit I find the message intriguing, especially as it arrives when I've jest finished writin' to the county attorney sayin' I can't attend.'

One yard apart, the two friends eyed one another very frankly.

' 'Imperative' is a rather unusual word for a young man like Gould to use, Dan. Can we be sure he sent the message, or do we have to think in terms of a trap?'

'I think he sent it, all right, Walter. The point is, who does he want me to meet?'

'So you're really contemplatin' goin' to the conference, on the say-so of this young fellow?'

'We employed him, didn't we, Walter? We have to show a bit of confidence in him when he makes a suggestion. After all, he's probably goin' to risk his life again over this matter at Silver Springs. Sure, I'm thinkin' of goin'. But I won't go alone. Neither will I alter one word of that letter already written to the county attorney!'

The tone of absolute conviction was back in the voice of the judge: one which had won for him many a court-room decision in his earlier days as an attorney. Vilman heard it and wished he had a voice like that himself.

'I guess Gould will be there, himself. As like as not he wants to point something out to you in the convention. Maybe he's got some evidence for you. The identity of the top man who has been your sworn enemy for so long.'

'You think *he* might be there?'

'It is certainly possible, old friend. I won't try to talk you out of goin' as you've already made up your mind, but I must admit I feel better since you said you won't go alone. Who do you think you'll take with you?'

'Two, maybe three first class guns. Men who learned their job in the army, I should think. Men with experience in security work who are not afraid to pull the trigger an' shoot straight in an emergency. Here, read what I put in the letter to Cyrus Quill. It'll help you not to get worried about my trip out of town.'

Vilman took the letter and read it. He knew the judge's style of handwriting and the smooth way in which he linked his ideas in sentences. Another sure sign of a sound legal training early in life. The letter started off cordially enough by asking about the health of the county attorney and his family. After that, the reluctant refusal to attend the convention, and the carefully worded explanation as to why Sherman could not conveniently attend.

He claimed to be working on the manuscript of a law book, which the publishers were pushing him to finish without delay. Sherman recalled a couple of earlier occasions when Quill and he had managed to mix business with pleasure to the joy of both, and concluded his letter with sincere wishes that the convention would be an outstanding success.

Vilman chuckled. 'You're a cunnin'

rascal, Dan. You're sendin' this letter by ordinary mail, tellin' everyone who knows Quill intimately that you can't possibly be there, an' all the time you are plannin' to turn up unannounced, actin' on the whim of a youngster half your age.

'Some folks would say you are devious, Dan. But I would say you seem to have a built-in survival kit. You deserve to live your full span and die finally in your own bed.'

Shortly after the judge had left, Vilman's confidence in his friend's survival began to be slowly undermined, but he kept his forebodings to himself.

* * *

Sam Gould spent a few days away from the cabin by himself. He went fishing, shooting and riding, revelling in the notion that Weldon had full confidence in him. Without that, he felt his nerve would have crumbled long before the time of the convention in Silver Springs. The time of waiting to know if the strike was on or off, nevertheless, punished his nervous system, and he found that he had to keep luring his thoughts back to Conchas City and his all-too-brief meeting with Melissa.

Weldon reappeared at six o'clock one evening, riding hard and belabouring his mount with rowel and whip, a sure sign that he was tremendously excited about something. This time, any one of his minions could have guessed what had put him in the enthusiastic mood.

'Howdy, boys,' he called, before he reached the cabin, 'don't go far away! Give me time to clean up a little, then we'll talk! The strike is *on*! The judge has written to say he won't be attendin', but he is makin' preparations which can only mean that he *is* intendin' to make the trip, after all!'

Jake Mayo walked two hundred yards through timber to get within hailing distance of the creek where Sam was fishing. One brief two-finger whistle, plus a wave and the sticking up of a thumb told Sam all he wanted to know of the sudden development. He waved back, rose to his feet as though he was keen to get back indoors, and tried to examine his thoughts.

The .45 Colt, which he had practised with during his lone shooting expeditions, hung at his thigh. He knew that in ensuring that the judge was going to make the trip to Silver Springs he had placed the retired legal man in a position of danger.

Sherman's survival would depend upon timing, after his arrival. And the Colt revolver swinging at Sam's hip. He would be the one man on the spot who knew the identity of all of the villains. His gun might very well have to be used. It might prolong the life of Melissa's father. As he brooded over the plot, Sam had the feeling that everything which had gone before in his life had been a preparation for what was to happen in the next few days. Everything else prior to this tricky escapade paled into insignificance.

Excitement brought him out in perspiration. He paused long enough to whip off his shirt by the water's edge and swish over his body a few gallons of water. He was the last to arrive at the shack, and Weldon was standing before a wall mirror checking on his appearance as he tucked in a clean shirt and studied the three men already seated at the table.

He said: 'Take a seat, Sam. I'll be with you in jest a minute. I can tell you that your puzzle message did the right thing. Sherman is plannin' to go to Silver Springs, even though he has written a polite refusal to the county attorney.'

Sam smiled at the rancher's reflection in the mirror. Mayo made room for him, and Danton indicated with a slight movement of his sparse brows that Sam could help himself to a small cigar. Presently, Weldon joined them.

He had a drawing of the court-house which showed in some detail the lay-out of the extensive ground floor and also indicated an upper gallery of seats at the south end which was linked along the west wall to the north end by a corridor.

Weldon spread out the plan carefully and gestured for the others to gather round the table and study it.

The main east-west thoroughfare of Silver Springs, known as Lincoln Avenue, flanked the southern aspect of the court-house, and the main entrance for the public lay on that side. Inside, and on the right, walled off from the main seating area, was an ante-room. This corner room connected with a corridor also walled off from the seating and leading all the way to the north end. In the north-east corner was a wash-room linked to the judge's private chamber by the north wall. From the chamber a private door gave access to another cross street named Jefferson.

Weldon stabbed a blunt forefinger at the bench, rigged crossways, a few yards in from the judge's chamber.

'That's where all the talkin' is done, boys. The legal men who are comin' to listen will use the main door in the south wall. I shall want Sam to greet the judge on arrival, usher him into the ante-room an' bring him straight down the corridor to the other end on some pretext.

'You, Joe, with Jake to back you, will have hidden yourselves in the wash-room. As soon as Sherman appears, you'll grab him, smuggle him out through the judge's private entrance and into the street. I'll be waiting there with a conveyance to spirit him away. Any questions?'

Sam whistled to hide his nervousness. Little Joe queried whether there was a window in the wash-room, received a positive answer and a lot of excited conjecture broke out, terminated by Danton.

'So far, Mr Weldon, you've made no mention of me. What do I do all this time? Take care of the reins?'

Weldon shook his head, and toyed

with his beard. 'See these dotted lines? They indicate the gallery. I'm not sure whether it will be occupied on such an occasion as this. Doc, I want you to hide yourself in this upper corridor down the west side. You'll be able to look down on the bench and the conference seats from there.

'In the event of Sherman refusin' to take the route Sam indicates, or any sort of setback with the judge in the main chamber, you are to shoot him an' shoot to kill! Is that understood? You're our second line of attack. A safeguard, if you like.'

Danton nodded, showing no emotion. 'What if the peace officers get wind of us?'

Weldon shrugged. 'You're a top professional, Doc. That's why you'll be there. If there's a commotion, fire off a few shots. Distract the lawmen, an' then get out the best way you can. I'll suggest a rendezvous later.'

'When do we go?' Sam asked.

'We start tomorrow morning. The

conference starts at noon, the day after that. An' I'm gettin' thirsty again. Let's open up a new bottle.'

Sam, having soaked up all the detail of the intended strike, drank as much as the others. He retired to his bunk hoping that he would not talk in his sleep.

15

The buckboard which had transported Judge Sherman from Conchas City was pulled by a couple of matching roan horses on this critical occasion. The judge, himself, held the reins and looked at his gold hunter watch. He chuckled, and glanced sideways at Jed Roder, the oldest son of the rancher on whose territory the judge and his daughter now resided.

'Exactly twenty minutes to midday, gents, an' who could have done better than that for timin', I ask you?'

Roder was a thick set, taciturn individual in his late twenties. He was of average height, and wore a tall undented dun stetson after the manner of his father, who also liked to look taller. Jed knew the judge well enough to grumble at him.

'I don't see any cause for merriment,

judge,' he grumbled, his left hand busy with the lush black moustache which covered his short upper lip. 'An' that goes for the other two, Willie an' Link. You ought to recollect that the conference itself starts at noon. We shan't make it into town for another ten minutes.'

Willie Worth and Link Peters were mounted up on horseback, one riding either side of the conveyance, as they had done for most of the journey. Worth was a long, gangling man in his early thirties who shared his time between long stints of trapping and short ones of doing a waddy's duties on the Box R. He favoured a skewbald. Men said he could move like an Indian when he felt like it. His long curving sideburns, brown in colour, circled the angles of his jaw and only failed to connect at his chin by one inch.

Peters always wore dark clothes. He was a former shot-gun guard, a man of forty years who was always watchful. His skin had a bronze tint to it which perhaps explained why he had remained a bachelor all his life and held himself slightly aloof from his fellow men. Not many men ever ventured to suggest to his face that he had a touch of Indian blood, but he could tell what they were thinking by the looks on their faces. Judge Sherman was one of the few men in the States entirely trusted by Peters.

'That'll be time enough,' Sherman returned, speaking more loudly. 'I know the three of you don't have a whole lot of confidence in young Gould, but *I* do have. I expect him to contact us as soon as we pull up outside the court-house. Jest keep your eyes skinned, an' act like you're supposed to be, constables of Conchas City out on a special assignment.

'I want you to remember that this young fellow is leadin' a double life at this moment. Who it is I'm supposed to meet is a matter for conjecture. But danger, figuratively speakin' is jest round the corner. Be prepared to fall in with any suggestion he makes. His an' my life may well depend upon it.'

There was a murmuring among the escort, each man in his own way confirming his allegiance to the judge. They became silent as other, slower vehicles ahead of them checked their pace and made them one of a column of visitors entering the town.

★　★　★

There were half a dozen deputies and constables on duty at the main entrance to the courthouse. Their duties ranged from welcoming VIPs to moving on their conveyances into the big temporary parking space down the west side of the imposing stone-faced building. At five minutes to noon, Sam Gould came out of the foyer closely on the heels of local Deputy Marshal Horace Bosco. Bosco was a tall, military figure with a brown waxed moustache, who had served as a peace officer in the county seat ever since he left the cavalry ten years earlier.

Bosco was responsible for recognizing the VIPs and therefore he was at times a little impatient with anyone who claimed his attention unnecessarily. Sam was a nervous case, had been for nearly half an hour.

'Now look you here, Gould,' Bosco remarked, turning sharply, 'you're still doggin' my heels. I can have you moved on any time I wish. I still don't believe Judge Sherman will turn up, an' I'm certainly not takin' any sort of instructions from you, if he does.'

Sam refused to be admonished. 'Would you take orders from me if Dan Sherman said it was vital?'

Bosco snapped his fingers under Sam's nose and deliberately turned away. A minute later, Dan Sherman arrived, beaming and waving his hand to both Bosco and Sam at the same time. Bosco looked baffled, but only for a few seconds. Sherman leapt down, shook him by the hand, and asked in a whisper if Bosco had made the acquaintance of Gould.

'I'm glad you've met, Horace. I figure there's an emergency of some sort on. Gould is my man. Anythin' special you want done, Sam?'

Sam moved in close and touched his hat. 'I have to take you indoors, judge. Don't take a step without me, yet. We need your three guards in with us at the same time. Deputy, please have your men take away the buck-board an' the two ridin' horses.'

Bosco acknowledged. Worth and Peters had already dismounted. A special glance from Roder prompted Sam to ask them not to bring in rifles so as not to look too conspicuous. He recollected that his own saddled horse was the only animal tethered to the hitchrail on the east side of the building, and that the Winchester recovered from Mayo was there on view if any sneak thief had the audacity to go that close under the noses of so many lawmen.

Sam preceded Sherman and the three guards through the first door.

He whispered: 'You know the layout of this buildin', judge. I'm supposed to take you through the ante-room an' down the corridor to the chamber at the other end. That's where trouble awaits you. Your chief enemy, if you didn't know it before, is Hank Weldon, rancher an' former politician, of the Circle W, near West Flats. He's waitin' in the next street, Jefferson, in another buck-board. For you.

'There are three hired guns in this plot. Danton is upstairs, or should be. Little Joe Gafferty an' Jake Mayo are waitin' to jump you in the judge's chamber an' spirit you away.'

Roder, Worth and Peters, standing closely together inside the entrance, with only a high wooden partition separating them from the scores of gossiping legal men in the audience, were impressed by Sam's revelations and the seriousness of his manner.

Roder started to say: 'Why didn't you — '

Judge Sherman cut him short and

made them all listen.

Sam said: 'You, judge, go through into the ante-room right now. Either stay in there, or nip out through the window. There's one saddled horse in the intersection, if you need one. Mine.'

Sam waited for the judge to slip through the door, and then turned to the guards. 'You three are goin' to have to tackle Little Joe an' Jake Mayo. The plotters might even know at this instant that the judge is in the building. So there's no time to lose. I don't have to tell you that Weldon's men are highly paid killers.'

'Come to the point, Gould,' Roder urged him hoarsely.

'I want you to go to the left, here, move around the audience near that wall, so you'll be out of sight of the gunman in the upper corridor. Don't let anyone stop you. Burst right into that chamber an' shoot first. Good luck.'

Bosco had come in behind them, looking intrigued and more than a little suspicious, but he made no move to impede them. Roder, Worth and Peters took off their hats and walked off, one behind the other, while Sam hovered by the ante-room, occasionally glancing upwards in an effort to locate Danton's position. During the whole of these preliminaries, the noise of gossiping lawyers and others connected with the legal profession spiralled to a crescendo.

Sam stepped into the ante-room, checked that the judge had not gone into the corridor, and noted the window, which was open. He decided to wait. The suspense punished his nerves.

★　★　★

Two minutes later, Jed Roder kicked open the door at the rear of the bench which gave access to the judge's private chamber. He dived through and went to his right, on one knee. Gafferty and Mayo were about eight feet apart, a pair of revolvers already drawn in each of their formidable hands.

Still on his knee, Roder threw up his Colt and blasted off at Gafferty, removing his hat, but leaving him otherwise unscathed. Willie Worth dived in through the open door and hurled himself to the left. He was not quite quick enough to avoid Mayo's quick retaliatory fire. The man who had killed Grout fired off both his guns at the same time, aiming one at Jed and the other at Worth. Because he was taken by surprise, and also attempting to hit two widely separated targets, he was not quite as accurate as usual.

The bullet fired at Roder singed the latter's bandanna and buried itself in the woodwork of the wall. The second, however, struck Worth high in the left shoulder and accelerated his dive, so that he hit the side wall on the left with stunning force.

Link Peters, who had the unenviable task of going in last, had to face both Gafferty's weapons. Peters fired his one gun hastily, and missed. Little Joe's discharging pieces were both on target.

The first grooved the ex-shotgun guard's right hip, while the second penetrated his heart, knocking him backwards through the door.

Roder rolled to his right. The low desk in the centre shielded him from Gafferty for a vital second or so, while he lined up on Mayo, holding his revolver steady with both hands. Roder's first shot hit Mayo in the thigh. A second was better aimed, ripping into his chest and dropping him backwards, already dying.

Gun smoke eddied in the small room, spilled out into the conference chamber: the echo of shots boomed and rattled the windows, effectively putting an end to all the lighthearted banter between the visitors who had so recently come together.

Having accounted for Mayo, Roder quickly scrambled to his feet. At the same time, Little Joe Gafferty, showing an agility rare in one of his bulk, dived in a prone position across the top of the low desk holding both his guns in front of him. Roder fired hastily and before he could loose a second shell, he was looking down the muzzles of the twin guns, which lanced flame. Both bullets struck him in the body. He reeled back and fell dead, in a crumpled heap across the body of Mayo.

For a second or two, Little Joe stayed where he was, his ears ringing with the shooting, his eyes blinking in the smoke. As the ringing noise abated, he found himself hearing his own raucous breathing. He put down a foot, came to his feet with both guns still at the ready and cautiously examined Roder and Mayo. Having kicked the inner door shut, he crossed to Worth and decided that he was dead, or very nearly dead.

Through the window, he could see Hank Weldon sitting holding the reins of his buckboard. The rancher was obviously startled, but he looked to be alert and ready for any further development. Gafferty's thoughts were slow to form. So far, the judge had not put in an appearance. Clearly, if the Boss was still waiting, he — Gafferty — ought to hold on a few seconds more and see if their quarry turned up.

He prowled the room, gradually getting his breath back, and wondering where Sam Gould had got to, and whether Danton was still in place at the upper level.

★ ★ ★

The sudden crash of gunfire took Sam's mind off the judge for a short while. He winced at the succession of crashes, and wondered at the outcome, his tortured imagination making him believe that all three of the guards up from Conchas might be dead. In something near panic, Sam negotiated the ante-room, ran along the corridor and only paused when he was entering the wash-room, located in the north-east corner.

He had his Colt in his hand without recollecting having drawn it. Gun smoke coming from under the door on the left tickled his nostrils and heightened his tenseness about what lay beyond. It seemed an age to him before he managed to call out in a dry constricted voice.

'Hey, you in there! Hold your fire! This is Sam Gould! I'm comin' through!'

He kicked the door, which opened under the pressure and allowed him to advance into the room of the carnage. The first thing he noticed without actually looking down was the twisted heap made up of Mayo's and Roder's bodies. Little Joe was standing in a gunman's crouch on the far side, half way between the inner door and the window facing onto the street.

Sam saw the blood oozing from Worth's wound in the far corner and his expression altered. The number of times he had experienced rage with a gun in his hand were limited. On this occasion, Little Joe, who had already suspected treachery and earmarked Sam as the most likely person to be playing a double game, saw the change in his expression.

As soon as the redhead's gun hand moved, Joe prepared to retaliate. Joe's right hand gun erupted first, although Sam appeared to fire simultaneously. The latter felt a tug at the left side of his waist as Gafferty's bullet touched his waistbelt. At the same time, Sam's bullet homed into Little Joe's chest, high on the right side.

Gafferty's second weapon erupted as he was spun around by the force of the bullet entering his chest. Sam avoided it, although he was much too slow to have moved in time. The big balding outlaw then sank down on all fours, gasping for breath.

Sam moved cautiously around the desk, went up behind him and kicked away from him the deadly twin weapons which were only loosely gripped at the time. Gafferty's head sank lower and his general appearance suggested that he was no longer a menace.

Sam backed off, breathing hard. A single glance through the window was sufficient to show that Weldon was still there, waiting patiently on the box of the buck-board. The rancher's attention seemed to be focused on something or someone out of doors and nearer the intersection.

Sam wondered a lot about that. Only one thing could keep Weldon there in a vulnerable position when it was clear that something had gone radically wrong with his latest scheme. The chance that the judge might still be eliminated.

Where was the judge? Had he availed himself of the single saddled horse adjacent to him in the intersection, or had he gone for a brief walk until the lethal exchanges were over? Sam's thoughts alternated between the judge and Weldon, his chief enemy.

Gafferty's laboured breathing failed to draw his attention. Instead, the redhead stepped out of doors into the street, his revolver held down at his side. There, he saw a remarkable situation. Judge Sherman had moved across from the intersection and was heading straight for the buckboard and Weldon.

The two enemies both witnessed Sam's arrival on the street. Weldon was acting as though he had the whole situation well in hand. Sherman was heading straight towards him, his back upright like that of a military man. The judge's small paunch was well pulled in under his tailored grey jacket, and Sam thought he detected a gunbelt at his waist, worn perhaps a little higher than was usual among gunmen.

Feeling like a bit part actor at a performance, Sam wondered what to do next. Somewhere in the background was Doc Danton, a gunman even more deadly in his opinion than Gafferty and Mayo. The judge still had to be protected. Sam dithered about for a few seconds and then did what seemed reasonable to him.

He ran to the intersection to collect his chestnut mount.

16

For a thousand dollars cash, a man who lived by the gun would accept orders without asking a lot of questions, provided that mistakes in the planning did not greatly reduce his own chances of survival.

Doc Danton, a man who in recent years had found it far more profitable to terminate men's lives rather than prolong them by the practice of medicine had his doubts about his own part in the plot to capture Dan Sherman right from the start. He was too far removed at the outset from the scene of the probable action.

However, as the action — if it developed unnecessarily — was likely to draw the law enforcement officers away from him rather than towards him, he did not offer any objections when Hank Weldon sent him upstairs to keep a vigil on the top corridor.

He knew as quickly as anyone that something had gone wrong. He had caught one brief glimpse of Sam Gould and the elderly ex-judge as they entered by the main door, and after that he had kept well out of sight until the sudden shooting started in the judge's private chamber.

He had his route for removing himself all worked out if anything went wrong. As soon as the first shooting exchanges occurred, he went along the open-sided corridor almost on all fours, heading for the end window in the west wall which he already knew to be open.

Fortunately for him, there were no visitors in the main gallery on this occasion and so no one saw him make his move. The great clamour in the enclosed space built up, and still the local guards and peace officers stayed where they were. He could have gone down the stairs in the north-west corner and dashed for the judges' chamber from that angle, but he preferred to keep himself away from the stunned delegates and the baffled peace officers who were supposed to be protecting them.

Exerting gentle pressure, he eased up the window and looked out. Beneath him on that side was the huge parking space, fully loaded with vehicles, and the hitchrails closer in towards the building. A few horses were snorting and fretting down there, but no humans looked up to see him emerge.

His head and shoulders came out first. He reached for a fall pipe, two feet to one side, hauled out his legs and held onto the pipe like a human fly. Half a dozen muscular efforts took him up onto the flat roof and then he was moving along the parapet towards the north-west corner and Jefferson Avenue.

★　★　★

As Sam mounted up and nudged the chestnut into life, the street door of the judge's chamber opened once more.

Little Joe, working hard to make his eyes focus and with one side of his shirt crimson, flopped on one knee and very nearly toppled over.

Joe called: 'Danton? Danton, where are you? Watch out for Sam Gould! He's changed sides! You hear me?'

In ordinary times, Gafferty's call would have alerted half the street, but now his fruity voice was feeble and even as he shouted his warning he had doubts as to whether it would carry sufficiently strongly. He did not see Danton, and his attention was taken by the approaching horse as Sam came round the corner and sent the chestnut for the buckboard.

At the same time, Weldon stirred his two horses and put the conveyance in motion. For a few vital seconds an air of unreality encompassed the two enemies. Sherman had scrambled up beside Weldon as though they were close friends and this was an everyday occurrence.

A wolfish expression told of Sam's

anxiety as he put his horse between the crouching figure of Gafferty and the other two up on the box. A slight scrambling, scraping noise almost passed unnoticed as Danton dropped down from the parapet of the court house roof and alighted rather unsteadily on a two-foot wide narrow stone ledge half way up the end of the building.

As soon as he had recovered his balance, Danton stuck his back against the wall and pulled his guns. Gafferty's uncertain eyes were groping towards the sounds he made. Sam Gould spotted the gunman at once, but it was Danton who first noticed the judge slipping his revolver out of its holster beside Hank Weldon.

Sam took his cue from Danton, who at once started to line up his weapons on the judge to protect Weldon. Rowelling the chestnut rather savagely, the redhead came close alongside of the conveyance and reached out with his right hand towards the judge, pushing him forcefully forward so that he lost his balance and almost toppled among the working hind hooves of the team.

Danton aimed both his guns at a spot high on the judge's chest, but the last minute lurch by the old legal man caused him to miss his target and hit the man directly beside him. The two bullets struck Weldon an inch or two above belt level, while Sherman tottered precariously with one leg trailing between the shaft on his side and the floor of the box.

The shaft horses accelerated, due to the shooting. The happenings of the ensuing few seconds occurred so rapidly that Sam had difficulty in recalling the order afterwards. The buckboard began to go away from him. Gafferty, whose left side still functioned properly, had brought one Colt with him.

Shouting hoarsely when his clearing vision revealed what had happened to Weldon, Little Joe lined up his gun on Sherman and tried to steady himself on one knee. Sam perceived what he was about and hastily loosened off a shot which finally killed Gafferty.

While Little Joe was sprawling on his back, Danton suddenly dropped to a sitting position on his ledge. Sam hauled the chestnut sideways, and fired up at Danton, but his aim was out. He chipped splinters out of the stone wall as Danton dropped to the dirt of the street.

The chestnut reared as Sam fired, spoiling his chance to finish off Danton as the latter landed heavily in the dust. Although he was clearly shaken, Danton rolled and hopped across the width of the street and dived into the building opposite through a door that gave as his shoulders hit it.

Sam heard himself using oaths which had never crossed his lips before. The buckboard had gone off up the street, with the judge more or less recovered and in charge. Two bullets had miraculously missed Danton before he disappeared from view.

Now, Sam had to dismount and go into the building after him, and that meant that the advantage of surprise lay with his adversary. He was thinking that Danton had a charmed life as he went through the door and pulled up short, stopped because his eyes needed time to adjust to the indoor shadows.

Sam was conscious of a lot of heavy furniture and drapes, but there was no sign of Danton. Rather belatedly, he dropped to the carpet, aware that he had been a clear target for anyone waiting for him. No shots came at him. There were two doors opening to other parts of the house from that one. Probably Danton had gone through one of them.

What next? Nothing could have startled Sam more than the sudden explosion of breaking glass. The pieces were still tinkling when a distant shout was heard. A man's voice. Probably someone at last emerging from the courthouse at the carnage end. A voice which sounded a continent away.

A few thudding footsteps and the unmistakable sounds to Sam's straining ears of a man getting to horse. He cursed again, went out the way he had entered and ran to the end of the building. He was just in time to see Danton, mounted up and turning a corner out of the alley between that building and the next.

The Doc had dived through a window, taking the glass with him, in order to get to his horse and put a safer distance under him. Or so thought Sam. The redhead backtracked again, shouting loudly for the chestnut which had wandered off a few yards.

His booted foot missed the stirrup the first time, and he had an awful feeling that this assignment was going bad on him. A couple of outlaws might have been eliminated, and their leader wounded, but that did not mean that Dan Sherman was safe.

The judge would have to manipulate the reins. That would leave Weldon free to get to his weapons. Wounded he might be, but an intense consuming hatred such as Weldon was fired with would maintain him long enough to achieve his greatest ambition, that of killing the judge. Perspiration, which had been spurting from Sam's head and trunk since the action began, started cooling rapidly. His shirt stuck to his shoulders.

After making a couple of turns, he had raised his hand to adjust his stetson when a bullet beat him to it. The bullet, fired from the sidewalk and the corner of a building, hit the brim at the front and lifted it off his head, regardless of the perspiration.

Danton, who was not simply thinking about a hasty retreat from town, moved on again, while Sam hauled the chestnut back into the shade and began to think about a running duel on horseback. More man-made noises from the court-house, but much too far off to play any part in a chase centred on the north and west of the town.

Dan Sherman's heart had thumped quite a bit as the outlaw's bullets went close enough to him to hit the man beside him. A good deal of effort from a man of sixty-eight years was required for him to resume his seat on the box and take the team under control.

Sherman turned the team to the right, and then to the left, his aim being to throw off any outlaw pursuit still within striking distance. Weldon had aimed one or two lethal glances at him, but the outlaw Boss's time was running out. He was literally leaking blood to his death, which could only be minutes away.

Having relieved him of his gun, Sherman glanced down at him and wondered if there was anything worth learning from his enemy before the latter expired. With his hands clasped to his waist, Weldon talked. His hatred ensured that. All his bitterness came out in his words. How he had failed to make any real headway in his first choice of professions, that of politics. How he had been outshone by a relation. He had slipped into villainy almost by accident. The smoothness of the first operation he masterminded had given him a new feeling of well-being. It had been all his work to plan, to gain intelligence of worthwhile coups, and to organise strikes, operating no less than three gangs at the same time.

All had gone well until a man on the right side of the law with an intelligence system as good as his own had started to build up a dossier upon the gangs, and also all known facts about the brains behind them. Dan Sherman had started to make so much headway that Weldon almost feared him and at once he thought of ways to hit out at the man undermining his system and his strikes against banks and other institutions.

Weldon coughed on blood, having lost count of the time that they had been riding together.

'I may leave you in this world, Sherman, but I took your son away from you an' that comfortin' thought I shall take with me to wherever it is I go next!'

More coughing, and a few hitherto unknown details about how the kidnapping was brought off, and how the boy's untimely death was ensured by Little Joe Gafferty acting directly under Weldon's orders. Sherman turned the buckboard yet again, and to his surprise a bullet followed them round the corner.

He was still marvelling and wondering who was within striking distance of them when Weldon totally unexpectedly made his last request.

'Get me offen the street!'

Sherman was blinking thoughtfully about possible pursuit. Maybe it would be a good thing to get off the street, if only for a short time. He recollected how attentive and effective young Sam Gould had been and his growing conviction was that Sam would not give up the pursuit of the buckboard.

The conveyance was heading south, along an intersecting street well to westward. Sherman drove across another avenue and turned right. A big double-fronted livery went by on his right, and then a big barn with its huge door invitingly open.

Weldon's death rattle was adding a faint extra to the cacophony of sound produced by the buckboard and the horses as the judge turned in and slowed the team.

*   *   *

From the bench of the speaker, Deputy Marshal Horace Bosco informed the assembled legal gentry of some of the facts which had delayed the start of the convention. For some time, apparently, Judge Sherman's life had been threatened by an old enemy. The shooting had been about the latest attempt on the judge's life. As far as the facts were known, Dan Sherman still survived.

All present were advised to stay. Some of the guard force was cautiously filtered away into the main thoroughfares. The local townsfolk were told to stay off the streets and keep their doors and shutters closed until further orders.

★　★　★

Long before Sherman took sanctuary in the barn, Sam was in a baffled state of mind. He had lost touch with Danton, and also with the buckboard and its double burden. He felt that Danton, having shot his Boss by mistake, would be equally keen to catch up with the judge and finish him off.

If Danton was still on the prowl, and there were no reasons to suppose otherwise, then both Dan Sherman and Sam himself were in perpetual danger. Sam faced up to this possibility, and yet his impatience overrode his judgement.

Within five minutes, he was riding this way and that, and openly calling the judge's name. 'Judge Sherman! Dan Sherman, if you can hear me at all, let me know where you are! This is Sam Gould, an' you may need more help yet!'

Sherman heard him when he had called three times. Weldon was dead, and in fact the old legal man did not like the stuffiness of the barn. He began to roll back the door, which was only used when excess animals from the livery were housed in there.

'Over here, Sam! In the barn! Hurry it up, will you?'

Sam was fifty yards away and Sherman had to shout a second time. Unknown to either of them, Danton was closer. He was in the act of exchanging his tired skewbald for a roan in tip top condition hitched not far from the livery among other horses. Danton, who had also lost track of the two principals in the action, half-straightened and showed quiet enthusiasm. Here was a last chance to influence the issue: one which he had just concluded was to be denied him.

There was little time for manoeuvre, especially as the judge was hovering in the entrance to the barn and about to step outside. Danton decided to use the hitched horses as his cover. He crouched behind them, intent upon taking the judge first. Sherman looked tired but somehow elated as he stepped into the open air and glanced up the street towards the plodding chestnut and its familiar rider. He produced a handkerchief and was in the act of blowing his nose when Danton fired his first shot.

The horses were startled, jerking to the full amount of distance permitted by their tethers. Equally startled, however, was Sam Gould, who hauled back on his reins and pulled his gun. Was there to be no end to this action? he wondered. Now, he was back in touch. If he wasn't both careful and lucky he was about to witness Sherman's death.

Already, the startled judge was

sinking to the ground . . .

Sam fired a shot between the legs of the tethered animals to keep Danton busy. He then headed the chestnut towards the other side of the street and leapt clear of leather. As his body sailed towards the sidewalk and the corner of the building, the chestnut absorbed a bullet in a vital spot.

Sam landed heavily and crawled out of sight. The horse rolled over once, not more than three or four yards away and then lay still with the butt of the Winchester pointing towards its owner, but still in the scabbard. To make matters worse, Sam had lost his grip on the Colt, which meant he was weaponless.

Caution, however, seemed to be a thing of the past. The judge moved sufficiently to show that he was alive. Danton, reading the situation well, slowly straightened up behind the horses and stepped clear to finish off the judge. Sam launched himself across the space between cover and the dead horse. A chance revolver shot flew over his head. He landed short, hurriedly crawled closer to use the dead beast as cover and succeeded in slipping the Winchester free.

Danton had both his revolvers lined up on the judge from ten yards away. He was about to do one of his celebrated double shots. Sam rested the Winchester across the saddle, hastily levered a shell into the breech and fired. Danton sprang about as if he had been startled. In fact, he had been hit, near the waistline. He fired his two shots into the leather of the saddle before Sam's second shot shattered his breastbone.

No more shooting. Danton was still settling down in a crumpled heap when Sam walked across to the judge and bent over him.

'It ain't bad, Sam. Jest a nick across the top of my right shoulder. Sit down, why don't you? I figure that shootin' will bring help in a minute.'

Sam slumped rather than sat. He

said: 'Shucks, judge, for a while I thought Melissa was goin' to be fatherless.'

★   ★   ★

A local doctor insisted that Dan Sherman should rest in Silver Springs for four days before attempting the long ride back to Conchas City. The judge grumbled, and Sam grumbled when Sherman was not around to hear.

However, the authorities in Conchas, along with Melissa, were informed in some detail by telegraph about the final clash between the judge and his enemies. To pass the time, the judge and Sam sat around and talked, exchanging lots of intimate details about their respective kin. Sherman suggested that Sam would have fine prospects when he got back to Conchas, and he pretended not to notice when Sam's scarcely veiled interest in his daughter came uppermost in the conversation.

On the evening before they were due to depart for home, Sherman expressed himself as being tired. Tired through age.

'Sam, there's something missin' out of my life. I've only jest realized what it is. I ought to have grandchildren. What do you think about that?'

Sam held his beer glass up to the light and appeared to be pondering the question. 'Seems like a good idea, judge. Only Melissa will figure in an such enterprise. Do you have any idea what sort of a man she would fancy for a husband?'

In his turn, Sherman examined his whisky glass. 'It rather depends on the fellow, Sam. I don't reckon she'd care if he worked on a ranch, or edited a newspaper, or ran a detective agency. Jest so long as he was truly attracted to her an' approved of by her Pa.'

Sam's fresh freckled complexion coloured up as he understood the broad hint which was being given to him.

He sounded a bit naive, as he answered.

'Strange you should touch on those particular jobs, judge. I only know one fellow who could possibly combine them all, an' that's me!'

Sherman subsided into laughter which slightly troubled his right shoulder and the supporting sling.

'Well, Sam, you'll have to do the courtin' when we get back, but you can take it her Pa will approve. Drink up an' fetch some more.'

THE END

A TOWN CALLED TROUBLESOME

John Dyson

Matt Matthews had carved his ranch out of the wild Wyoming frontier. But he had his troubles. The big blow of '86 was catastrophic, with dead beeves littering the plains, and the oncoming winter presaged worse. On top of this, a gang of desperadoes had moved into the Snake River valley, killing, raping and rustling. All Matt can do is to take on the killers single-handed. But will he escape the hail of lead?

RODEO RENEGADE

Ty Kirwan

When English couple Rufus and Nancy Medford inherit a ranch in New Mexico, they find the majority of their neighbours are hostile to strangers. Befriended by only one rancher, and plagued by rustlers, the thought of returning to England is tempting, but needing to prove himself, Rufus is coached as a fighter by a circus sharp shooter, the mysterious Ghost of the Cimarron. But will this be enough to overcome the frightening odds against him?